I0667520

IN THE
SNOW GLOBE

Damian Pasieka

MONTAG

First Montag Press E-Book and Paperback Original Edition April 2023

Copyright © 2023 by Damian Pasieka

As the writer and creator of this story, Damian Pasieka asserts the right to be identified as the author of this book.

All rights reserved. No part of this book may be reproduced or transmitted in any form or by any means, electronic or mechanical, including photocopying, recording, or by any information storage and retrieval system without the written permission of the author, except where permitted by law. However, the physical paper book may, by way of trade or otherwise, be lent, re-sold, or hired out without the publisher's prior consent.

Montag Press ISBN: 978-1-957010-27-4
Design © 2023 Amit Dey

Montag Press Team:

Cover: Rick Febre
Editor: Charlie Franco
Managing Director: Charlie Franco

A Montag Press Book
www.montagpress.com
Montag Press
777 Morton Street, Unit B
San Francisco CA 94129 USA

Montag Press, the burning book with the hatchet cover, the skewed word mark and the portrayal of the long-suffering fireman mascot are trademarks of Montag Press.

Printed & Digitally Originated in the United States of America
10 9 8 7 6 5 4 3 2 1

This book is a work of fiction. Names, characters, places, and incidents are either products of the author's vivid and sometimes disturbing imagination or are used fictitiously without any regards with possible parallel realities. Any resemblance to actual persons, living or dead, events, or locales is entirely coincidental.

To my grandfather, Jan Auguściak

PART ONE

PECCATORES

THE INTERROGATION

Have you ever had to leave a place you love?
Imagine you can't see your home anymore. You may say that the whole world is your home, but that's not true. Those few streets around may be more important for you than a cultural revolution. By destroying the roots, you destroy yourself. I know the world is constantly changing, but not everywhere.

Time seems to have stopped on Stars street. Nothing remarkable has happened here for years, and other city citizens have forgotten this corner a long time ago. The elderly inhabitants of the block of flats live in an atmosphere of blissful peace, surrounded by their old porcelain tableware and by the crystal vases that were fashionable decades ago, all of them covered with dust that remembered the time of the first moon landing. Only the decanters were taken out and displayed on the special occasion of family Christmases or birthday parties. On other days, visits from relatives hardly happen. The only regular visitors are an elderly postman and the shadows of birch trees streaming through the windows. The black and white bark makes me think of the cinema of years gone by when everything was more real and somehow simpler.

Every day is almost the same as the day before. In the morning, the stream of sleepy people slowly spills out of the staircases. They rub their eyes to devote themselves to their routine duties. In the afternoons, the air vents smell of fried, sizzling meat and dill-roasted potatoes. Finally, in the evenings, there is complete silence. Were it not for the street lamps, it would seem that the whole world disappeared, so as not to bother anyone else with its existence. This sleepy, collective life continues until the day my story happens. It disturbs the dreams of my neighbors for a long time.

What's my name? Although I much prefer my full name, people call me Stan. Yes, it's me who killed the scumbag... this worthless bastard who brazenly adored my daughter. I was stoic when I dispensed the proper justice. No one else would have dared to do what I have done... punishment that needed to be done. I have always detested passivity and observing from a safe distance. This type of reaction is an unwritten local tradition. It seems that this applies not only to my surroundings but to the whole of the nation.

Do I regret it even a little bit? Not really. I would do it once again, although it didn't bring me any satisfaction. I'm an honorable man. My honor is all I have left after the humiliations that befell me. Even though it has only been a few or a dozen days, my memories of them are not clear. So far, I am frustrated by the insolence with which I was treated. However, I have to state that I didn't expect anything else in the situation in which I found myself.

They dared to lead me to a room with a one-way mirror as to Golgotha. Among them were the hateful rogues, adorned with faded ink and scars, their faces looking like dead ones and I felt utterly disgusted. The only fear I had was that my face might turn out to be the same and I am just as delusional about my own humanity. However, it seems doubtful to me, as I knew the reason for my presence in this place. I don't blame it on any fate and I don't blame myself for not being smart enough as well. Moreover, I don't regret that I was captured, which was not to be said for the rest of the rotten criminals that surrounded me.

My private Way of the Cross had been going on for years. However, I didn't fall under its weight even once, and I didn't receive even the slightest consolation from the gathered crowd. Simon of Cyrene was not forced to help this time, no one wiped my face marked with traces of past experiences. Perhaps only my daughter did, though I always tried to protect her from the awareness of the horrors of this world. She did not deserve even the slightest bit of such trouble.

Milena, my daughter, is a child of political breakthrough and transformation. Her childhood was at the time when the wild capitalism reached us. It changed the rules of the game and gave us hope for a better future. Nobody scared children with the black Volga anymore[1], and bright colors popped up everywhere like in a kaleidoscope. Fortunes were made in a year and lost even faster. The times of the ubiquitous bazaars, where in the open air, under striped tents around the speed-way stadium, you could buy everything. There were available

---

[1] In Poland, naughty children were threatened with being kidnapped by the devil driving a Russian car.

such abstractive products as the bootleg cassette tapes, massive fox furs, gas pistols, and Soviet medals from World War II. The exchange offices grew like mushrooms after the rain, one next to the other filling the entire street next to the philharmonic hall. This is where my uncle met his unpleasant fate. But that is a completely different story that I will not discuss here.

Cars from western factories, our first personal computers with floppy drives, and holidays abroad. We were enchanted by the freedom, not fully prepared for it. We rushed tirelessly, trying to build something new on the ruins of the old system, but it didn't last long. It was in the midst of all this colorful chaos that my daughter was brought up. Her childhood was completely different from mine, even though not so many years had passed.

I couldn't let her feel even a little pain or anxiety because of my problems. It's enough that I had to atone for the sins of people who, due to the various social or genetic bonds, should be close to me. Probably many will think that I exaggerate, but still, I cannot forget the events of my childhood. They remind me to learn from someone else's mistakes instead of repeating them endlessly.

How did it used to be in my early childhood? My parents and I lived in a place that consisted of one flat and three separate worlds. Nobody came to visit us, never. Perhaps only a nosy neighbor dared to peer through the crack of the ajar door to feed his insatiable eyes. Our terrible Tower of Babel tried to reach for heaven. From the outsider it looked majestic, radiating a calm glow. Inside it was disgusting, twisted, and fully dehumanizing. Even though we still spoke one language, we couldn't talk to each other. There were no conversations at all, all of dad's desperate efforts were in vain. Thanks to my mother, there was only a deathly silence, broken by interrogations. My father and I remained silent despite our good intentions. This silence brought me out of the land of muteness, out of the house of bondage. It lets us bless the oblivion.

This is how it used to be, but now the last station of my Way of the Cross seems to be approaching with great strides. There is no longer any chance of turning back, it is a real standoff. As I mentioned, no one helped me to carry my cross along my way. I don't even want to think about asking anybody for help. I am too proud, though sometimes I wonder if it was a mistake, but doubts disappeared as soon as they arose. I don't know if someone's advice could change anything about this whole mess. I've received too many of them already. The only thing I know is that I feel violated.

Although to some this may seem absurd, the presence of a suspicious company of criminals made me feel innocent. The crime I committed could have been done by any of them, they were simply created for that purpose. They were full of anger and meanness. They used someone else's good nature by deception, but it was me who had to face the unpleasant consequences. To be honest, these consequences couldn't make any impression on me after all that has happened to me, which I will tell you about it later. I was a dead Man walking. Meanwhile, the eyes of my compulsory companions gleamed ominously, the same as the knife I stuck in this scumbag at the moment of my final triumph. That was the moment when rough waves of blood surged and carried me unconsciously to this lousy place where I am kept locked and observed continuously.

During my summer walks, I have passed this place hundreds, if not thousands of times. However, so far, I have visited this gloomy, overwhelming place only once, and it was only because of the primary school I attended. This type of excursion used to be an obligatory element of education. As a preventive measure, it was intended to scare the children. In those days, adults liked to scare children at every turn.

The monumental building of the police station is located just a few blocks from where I lived. Most of these blocks are filled with student dormitories and a university of technology that remembers better times. These buildings are in stark contrast to the average age of the local citizens, most of whom were retired or had almost reached the necessary age to stop working. The most characteristic building is a large wave-shaped block of flats. From early childhood, it seemed to me a self-sufficient anthill. What was inside? There are tailor shops, a haberdashery, a bakery, microscopic grocery stores, a kiosk, and probably more than a few places hidden from undesirable visitors. You could get lost in its meandering passages and tunnels of interconnecting cellars. It is a real labyrinth. The pinkish sidewalk that runs parallel to the apartment block is also wave-shaped, which could make many pedestrians seriously dizzy – ascending and descending, steps and ramps for the wheelchairs, bumps, and missing pavement stones.

All the anomalies end abruptly to restore the regular shape of the street, which runs perfectly in the rest of its parts. The very edge of our small perceptual bubble is marked by a wide artery, the pope's avenue, that separates us from the representative part of the city. Almost all well-known law firms, courts, and official buildings are located in its vicinity. They are immersed in the maze of pre-war Jewish tenement houses full of cafes, gates, and unexplored alleys. Everything is dominated by the monastic tower for which my hometown is known. The tower regularly hides behind the different buildings, only to reappear after a while and navigate the lost wanderers.

It is the time, however, to focus on the building of the police station. I never thought that I would visit it again and that it would take place under such unpleasant circumstances.

We were herded and numbered just like cattle, staying one next to the other in a room of approximately two by three meters, five people shoulder to shoulder. I was disgusted to breathe the same air as they did. Even worse were the accidental touches and soft, gentle rubbings against the hot sweaty male arms that caused unforgivable harm to the innocent victims. I felt a strong, even desperate need to wash away this dirt and disgrace. However, there was no such possibility, so, nervously, I rubbed my hands on my legs as if it could bring relief to my situation. I rubbed harder and harder with passion, trying not to let anyone notice it. Nothing brought any relief, and the disgust grew in me to a breaking point but I knew I had to survive, being stuck with atoms of someone else's filth and desire.

Perhaps the most surprising fact is that it was only the touch that made me anxious, and not the process itself in which I participated and which in the next few moments was to bring me to my final ruin. Five pairs of soles slid with nervous tics on the dark green linoleum surface. They followed the old smudges. The most significant signs of those times when the building was raised were the reinforced concrete, the paneling, and the gumoleum – the holy trinity. What is more? A musty smell that you cannot get rid of, even with the strongest German chemicals. There is no force that can remove it.

I missed open spaces. It was a strange feeling because I lived in a block of flats since I was little and it was my natural habitat. The longing for space was a false nostalgia. To catch my breath once more, to walk towards the distant horizon until my strength is exhausted, even if it meant the very end of the world or my own. To be like my ancestors in footwraps and thick, ragged coats. To travel east, to the land of eternal frost and red noses, a forgotten purgatory among frozen rivers, with only a few poor thatched houses around and an endless emptiness. Has this land ever really existed or was it just a dream or a collective imagination among artists who fed us with similar visions? The call of nature and daily hunting to survive the next day. No, it was too irrational, an idiotic idea, the mind creating infantile visions to pass the time. The contradictions started to irritate me, once again.

The second thought, for some reason, was about the church I attended as a little boy. I thought of its wide naves and the blistering cold of the dark granite floor. There were colorful stained-glass windows, thick lenses that let through only a fraction of the refracted rays. These rays traveled lazily across the floor as the liturgy progressed and reminded the faithful of the sign of the covenant. During the sacrament, they huddled timidly against the wall. During the sermons, they dazzled the eyes and reflected from the thick glasses. Everything seemed to fulfill the eternal plan. Portraits of anonymous Saints with long, gray beards and long faces full of wisdom peeked from the walls. The scent of all parishes is the same - incense, the lavender aroma from time-worn fur, and highly fragrant old women's perfumes that have caused more than one fainting. And that one beautiful perfume of an unknown woman that I could inhale for hours. They were named after Napoleon's lover, which I found out by accident years later. I stared with fascination at the gaps in the vault, from which the dim light emanated as I was looking for God. We, the ecclesial community, the saints, the perfumes, and in front of us the tabernacle and the mystery of existence. Now I could fear a different community, no longer having much to do with childlike purity of thought.

I would like to tell you more about the room in which I was locked, but all my attention was drawn to the sight that was right in front of me. This was a picture full of secrets – my face. The one I looked at in the bathroom every morning, in the damp, foggy mirror while shaving, which always bored me. I have seen it hundreds of thousands of times, but I have never looked at it that closely for a long time. My face was usually hidden behind the snow-white foam that was applied with the same old brush as itself. Now it had nothing to hide behind, so, naturally, it caught my eye. It was the first time I was examining the details, looking for some evidence. I was examining it from every side, in every ridge and crevice. Initial fears didn't materialize. It still didn't look like the faces of the rogues, or maybe that was just my subjective opinion and there wasn't much difference between them. The delicate wrinkles that had surrounded my eye sockets for several years remained invariably in their place, forming a delicate cobweb or a map. It's customary to say that these are the lines of laughter. It's not always a true statement. Except for those few furrows, my face looked young for its age, and despite the lack of plumpness and prominent cheekbones I realized that so far, I hadn't noticed the progressive gray hair on my head, which was gradually displacing the blackness of the slightly wavy, matted hair. But this didn't cause me the slightest concern. I used to have other problems on my mind.

I don't remember ever worrying too much about physical passing as far as I was concerned. Coming to terms with aging, surprisingly, came naturally to me. Something I rarely observed among my peers, the store shelves full of irritating, greasy creams for any time of the day. My generation kept buying them believing in miracles. Real nature was completely alien to them; it was an inhuman abstraction viewed from a distance on their tiny screens flickering in the night. Another issue for me was the passing of my loved ones, but it's not a significant issue in this story, so let me leave it in silence temporarily. It will be much easier this way.

If not old age, then what was I afraid of? I was afraid of many things, I'm not as brave as it may appear at first.

Perhaps this will cause a lot of surprises, but I remember, for example, that as a child, my greatest fear was the possibility that the universe is either an infinite or finite space, but still expanding. Both options were beyond the scope of a child's imagination. Many times, I had been unable to sleep, thinking for hours about the above theories and feeling like an insignificant grain in the great desert of space. I felt like a lonely, dying star, hidden behind a nebula, impossible to see through the lenses of any telescopes. I decided to fight it at all costs, but I had no idea where to start, unfortunately, and so it took years. The desire for meaning, action, immortality, and sick ambitions impossible to fulfill was my daily bread. The above expectations weakened over time to expire almost completely in adulthood and give place to another desire – a desire for uninterrupted peace. This goal turned out to be even more difficult to achieve, even impossible, especially in the place where I was brought up.

Only a one-way mirror separated me from a poor woman who was supposed to indicate me as if they were afraid that I would choke her without scruples. She was like a guardian of morality who stands at the window and selflessly watches over public order. She didn't sleep a wink at the sense of duty that gave her the last semblance of excitement that might be achieved in old age. She was the one eavesdropping with a chipped glass placed against the wall and a bloodshot eye to her peephole. She was the one who believed in the sanctity of her mission to the end, which she gave herself because of being bored with her life and its prolonged loneliness. What is more, she didn't even ask for thirty pieces of silver.

There was not a share of this infamous power of deduction in it, just obsession and paranoia. A dirty snitch, that stupid old prick.

This is how I thought about her at the beginning. Anger tends to block rationality at first in such situations. After a while, I came to my senses, because she was Innocent and with her state of knowledge, I would probably do the same if I was a witness. I couldn't resent her anymore, though I tried to do it. I realized that would be sheer hypocrisy.

I knew very well what was about to happen. It was not a lottery, just a matter of formalities. Formalities that were completely unnecessary because I had no intention of withholding the truth. Maybe I just wanted to hide the truth about myself and my emotions.

Suspect number two? To the front of the line,

this command, uttered in a hoarse, impassive voice reached my ears and I already knew how it would go on. I had just become a number; everything was now binary. The rest of the suspects, despite the lack of any reason, nervously decoded their mirrored numbers to make sure that this was their lucky day.

Hundreds of times I had seen similar scenes in the films. Over a dozen times I had read about them in my books. More than once they touched me or moved me in some strange, inexplicable way, but the real, private, the one I experienced myself, seemed to me the most ordinary and dispassionate of all of them. It was completely devoid of romanticism and sublime pathos. Let no one believe that I have sociopathic or similar personality disorders. There are no marks to suggest there is anything wrong with me, although I must admit that sometimes, especially in moments of weakness, I ineptly wish to become someone indifferent. It would have been a much easier path.

The verdict was passed unanimously, although it was not legally binding yet. She recognized me without the slightest hesitation. I was not surprised at all. There was no room for doubts. The whole recognition process lasted several seconds, up to half a minute, but it might have been enough to influence my whole future. Paradoxically, I felt a moment of relief. Soon I was about to free myself from the stuffiness and those disgusting touches, from that irritating, sharp smell of sweat, from those cadaverous faces, and their sinister, deadly stares. I took a steady and decisive step forward, like an exemplary parade participant or an experienced tightrope walker who takes the audience's breath away. However, there was no ovation for me. There was also no hope of an amicable settlement.

Everything was going in the wrong direction from the very beginning, although there was no possibility of my fall. I was too proud for that. I have constantly cultivated my pride, living in the conviction that if I don't respect myself, no one else will do it. I was brought up this way. Although I have often regretted many lessons that life has taught me, I have never dared to discuss it so far, it was always easier to hide everything.

So, this is not a nightmare or morbid dream, and a wild instinct has overcome all these supposedly sublime and noble values instilled in me from childhood. What filth.

No work above the norm, no national good – only revenge, revenge, and blood dripping in small streams onto the icy, mud-smeared floor of the staircase. Drip drip, drip drip, rhythmically like a march. A funeral march, in this case, that Chopin himself wouldn't be ashamed of it. I didn't regret my actions at all, and as I mentioned before, I didn't regret the fact that I was captured so quickly. I was able to look calmly at the dirty surface of the mirror, which stood between me and this elderly Pilate and reflected a figure full of self-control and coming to terms with the fate that had befallen him. Even if there were any emotions in me, I would never dare to show them. Who instilled in me this course of action?

Mother – a word associated with safety and selflessness, a rock in hard times. In culture it is an ideal image, even put on a pedestal. A single mother, our Mother Nature, Alma Mater, the court again gave full custody to the mother.

Crazy mother, how to love her? Screw it. She had been spying on me since I was a child, checking drawers every time and regularly turning my pockets inside out. The only thing she couldn't open and check was my head, even though she was quite close once. She diligently taught me, doing it constantly and consciously, so as not to show others even the slightest sign of weakness, because it would certainly be used against me in the future, at the least expected moment. The paranoid suspected deception and intrigues against her everywhere. Everyone was a potential cheat and thief to her, even me, her only son.

She suffered from another mania that was far more harmful than the first. *Man has to be solid as a rock. Crying is reserved only for suckers and losers. Nobody will like you if you are weak. Don't be a sissy, better take care of yourself* – she always repeated these to me when I had a moment of crisis, and it stuck deeply in my mind. What could she even know about it? Masculine mother, male mother, she probably dreamed of pissing standing up. It was not your fault, dad. Father, dad… my poor daddy. For every single stumble upon answering my mother's questions, I was severely disciplined or harassed. According to her, it was supposed to be the best educational method.

Fear of the dark – laughter.

Torn tooth – laughter.

Bruised knees – laughter.

First unhappy love – laughter, laughter, laughter.

It was so until my beloved grandfather died. At first, I cried for a long time, and then I made a long-awaited exodus to the promised land. Thirty-five square meters of good memories are always something good. The phone calls were disturbing me from time to time but I didn't answer. *I am not here, I do not exist, central, please keep it a secret, otherwise, I will not pay the bills. I am not joking.* The phone doesn't ring anymore. Silence, eternal silence. Until now, however, I sometimes hear my mother's voice in my sleep. These are the moments when my heart starts to beat faster and I cannot sleep peacefully afterward.

Her teachings lasted so long that twenty years after she passed away, I still couldn't completely shake off the habits of my childhood. I couldn't stop hiding my feelings, even though many times these secrets made me depressed and I wanted to shout them out to everyone around.

Only my beloved daughter, my little Angel, was able to persuade me to be honest in this field. For her, I agreed to an honesty that wouldn't burden her with any additional anxiety. This time she wasn't there with me, so I remained impenetrable. *Impenetrable* – how ridiculous it sounds. Others might take it as conceit or even pride and blame me for it. I couldn't, and I didn't even want to approach it differently. I didn't need pity. I despised it at the hands of strangers.

To my relief, the rest of the villains were finally led out of the room, and I remained alone. As I have mentioned, there was no clock or anything specific to talk about. There were only bare walls and the aforementioned mirror, which constantly attracted my attention from the lack of more interesting objects and activities. I had no idea if I was still being monitored and assessed. What is more, I had no idea what note would be issued to me. The times of sitting for hours in school rooms were long behind me and I didn't miss them a bit. *Please come to the blackboard right away. Oh, I can see you are unprepared. What a shame, what would your mother say? Sit down and button that top button!* – I felt similar at this point, but I struggled as much as I could to push this overwhelming mood away from me.

Loneliness even brought me a little relief. It was only temporary, but I couldn't expect more under all the circumstances. It seems to me that in isolation I waited quite long for any event, even a rustling outside the wall. Maybe they thought that they would break me with this forced confinement. It probably worked perfectly for many people overwhelmed with guilt or regret.

I must admit that one issue bothered me. All the time, I wondered what my poor Milena was doing. I wondered if she could handle this situation. All of these countless scenarios and thoughts swirled through my head. The inability to hide the deed from her was the only unforgivable mistake in the whole process. However, it could not be avoided. The world is full of injustice and meanness, especially for people as noble as her. She did not deserve to suffer. If I could only bear for her all the hardships she has ever faced. She was to be left alone, like an orphan, and I had promised myself it would never come to that. I wanted to do well in at least one thing in my life, and I had failed. I was hoping that she would not hate me for all of this, and in time she would understand that it was the only possible option for me to choose. I was hoping that she would forgive me and I would hold her tight as before, as I wanted to protect her from all the sorrows lurking in the unknown.

I snapped out of my reverie driving me into ever deeper melancholy mixed with nostalgia. Perhaps it was better, it was not the time for sentiment.

Two men in their forties in dark blue, crumpled uniforms stepped over me with hesitant and unsteady steps. They looked drunk. The condition of our uniformed service never allowed us to be sure about this matter – officers often tried to forget the drastic images that they had seen during their service. The pathology that gathered in the dark gates of tenement houses and apartments with piles of bottles and shabby plaster on the walls still terrified. It never changed and it is unlikely to change in the future, no allowances or community centers will help to solve this problem.

A long time ago, I stopped believing in all utopias, except those that I once stubbornly created during the next feeling of disappointment that was happening to me. Unevenly protruding collars only complemented the impression of professional burnout that had certainly hit them long ago, maybe even decades earlier. Despite their muscular figures, in the eyes of uniforms, I saw the panic and fear that can be seen in children who, against their own will and too early, enter the unknown world of adulthood. When drunk parents call, there is no choice; the same situation occurs when the state calls you – you have to proudly walk forward, even if it means that you go right into the abyss. This analogy seems very appropriate. In both cases a person tries to be mature beyond the measure, to push their limits with the risk of mental health impairment in the future, without any guarantee of the sense of their submissive actions. March, march, step by step – one step forward and two steps back. It's impossible to save the whole world, although many still make unsuccessful attempts and will make them more than once to finally burn themselves again and melt their Icarus wings. Probably it must remain that way. Despite the apparent causticity, I was once no better than all of them.

It seems that the limit of awkwardness has been exceeded and we stood there for too long without a word, overwhelmed by collective impotence or resignation. Although no one was in a hurry to leave, I noticed a twitch of the pressed corners of their mouths. The lips of both uniformed men moped slightly as if they were trying to peel off each other, but some secret force prevented them from doing so. Finally, they worked up the nerve and decided to communicate to me what I should do. No words were needed, I anticipated their intentions. I got up and followed them, knowing that unfortunately, it was time for more formalities.

Only a dozen or so meters of a completely straight gray corridor separated us from the interrogation room. It was the place where in one afternoon I would be expected to confess my innermost faults. There was only one problem, but perhaps quite significant, I still felt no guilt, much less a willingness to share anything with a person that I didn't know.

He was a Man just like me or, who knows, maybe more wicked, hidden only by the glow of his badge, a shield from the rest of society. How comfortable it must be to judge others ruthlessly while remaining an unexplored mystery. In such a case, anyone can pose as a righteous judge and an undefiled prophet. For this reason, from my early childhood, I avoided confessionals, they always felt inferior to me. This impression was intensified by the bars, which seemed to emphasize the distance between the mortal and the judging person. My hands trembled and my voice broke with nerves, which in the eyes of others could have been considered as a great sense of remorse, at a time when I just wanted to avoid the kangaroo courts, as confessions appeared in my vivid imagination. I preferred to confess to God personally. Without any intermediaries. It was in Him that I was looking for understanding and selflessness. The silence replacing the answer full of judgments and trite truisms did not bother me. I could feel the element of eternity in it, or maybe it was just my imagination again. However, it wasn't important at this point, although I was accompanied by the same silence as then. This time I wasn't looking for God or salvation in it. I sensed that it was only the calm before the storm that was to come.

On the way to the interrogation, no one said a single word to me, but I saw alternatively looks full of contempt and curiosity. Every onlooker fell silent, interrupting their earlier, animated conversations to focus their attention on me for a moment and make their silent judgment, which they shared with their companions as soon as I disappeared from sight. During this walk of shame, the only sound was the clatter of the heavy, military boots, with the hardened toes, the soles speaking with each step, provoking to give an answer. Their owners still had not uttered a single word, and nothing seemed able to break their conspiracy of silence. To this day, I am not sure whether this silence resulted from the requirement of the regulations, a psychological game, or the seriousness of the situation. One thing is for sure, I wanted to get it over with as soon as possible, no matter the results.

The short stroll, despite the completely stiff atmosphere, had allowed me to move my knees a little bit. After a while, we reached the interrogation room, which didn't seem to bring any relief to any of the three of us. The door swung open in front of me, emitting a long screech on its old hinges. It caused a great distress in the members of my forced escort, which was clearly visible. They looked at the floor, then the walls, waiting for the moment when all the formalities would be completed and they could leave with their conscience clear. Meanwhile, they had led me into a medium-sized room, which they quickly left. Their longed-for moment had come.

Inside the room, it was neither dark nor light, neither nice nor ugly. It was bland, as if a million other places where no one cares about the décor, but for the first time in a long period, I didn't feel bland.

During the surge of my imagination, a naive, purely megalomaniacal vision came to me. It was the vision that in a moment the battle for me would be fought by good and evil, virginity and beastliness, black and white. I imagined this event as a chess match between two grandmasters, in which no one can be sure of his victory, and each subsequent move of the figures takes place with due humility and respect for the entire ceremony, which was an art itself. With carefully concealed excitement, I awaited this eternal fight. I watched as my fingers trembled, looking forward to the result of this incident, which was to bring something fixed, unchanging, so longed for by me for a long period. I simply dreamed of elegant tailcoats and worldly manners, *savoir vivre* and resolute moves to tilt the scales of victory from one side to the other, delighting the audience with their insights.

Pride has led me astray.

To exaggerate is perhaps the most human thing in the world. An unpleasant confrontation with reality quickly followed, and no lance was crushed, no move was supposed to resemble a game of chess. Instead, a common man sat in front of me, as bland as the room itself, in which he used to work daily. He was the Man who also wanted to make me bland at all costs, to suck from me the remnants of what is extreme, haughty, and unnatural. People like him cannot bear any deviation from the norms written in all the regulations. They cannot even imagine them with the greatest effort of their will. Just one look and I knew that he wanted to make me one of them, those cogs in the machine of society, meaningless abominations that wander around thoughtlessly, waiting only to be turned into either bread or circuses, punctuated by advertisements for banks and drugs for bloating or potency. The detestation of the willing accepting mediocrity awakened in me.

Still, there was no escape from him, so I took refuge inside myself. My inside felt to be a larger and larger abyss, which widened with each passing moment more and more to absorb me piece by piece, inch by inch, and never again to let myself out onto the outside world, which at that moment seemed no less terrifying.

please sit down,

He didn't deign to introduce himself and, with a slightly curved finger of medium length, he pointed to an empty chair, and he sat down directly opposite. We were only separated by a table strewn with various hastily written papers and files that could only suggest how much time he had spent here that day listening to questionable testimonies of other delinquents. The handwriting looked like it had been written by a doctor, which effectively prevented me from reading even the pages that were within my reach. The owner of the notes was probably well aware of this because he didn't even try to hide anything from my sight. His hand itself was a perfect enigma.

According to his instructions, I was to sit on a neglected, wooden chair, which over the last fifty years has already hosted tens of thousands of people who sat on it for obvious reasons. It was a veritable throne of sin. Reluctantly, I obeyed. Just touching the backrest, I realized that it would be more comfortable to stand barefoot for even a few hours on the rough concrete floor below me. There weren't even tiles on the floor, just concrete, which, combined with the chair, only completed the picture of severity. An uncomfortable piece of furniture stuck in my back, reminding me about my spine, which had been strained in my youth making extra money loading and unloading the wagons. In an instant, a grimace reappeared on my face, but instinctively I managed to hide it before it was noticed.

It seems to me that the reason for the above behavior will not surprise anyone interested once he becomes familiar with it. It is rather trivial, let me explain. Our national investigative bodies, as well as probably all of their foreign counterparts, instinctively arouse anxiety even in a completely innocent person. Everyone knows what I am talking about and has experienced it at least once in their skin. The average passerby begins to monitor themself and behave completely unnaturally the moment that they see the uniform from a distance of several dozen meters. The hands stiffen, the back straightens automatically, and the heart picks up speed. Perhaps these are only my paranoid impressions from my youth and the few impressions I had after a face-to-face meeting with officers conducting environmental interviews. Please correct me if I'm wrong. However, I think that I was not completely alone in this, because I have often seen such a change in behavior among the passers-by around me. Even though their suddenly acquired stiffness made me laugh, I couldn't act otherwise. We continued on this game of appearances which served no purpose but only ridiculed us in front of one another. It is high time to get back to our history, however, at this point, I was also feeling somewhat stiff.

Can we start?

he asked me politely, though it was really obvious that I had no choice.

Yes, of course. Please ask.

Would you like a glass of water? I'm not sure how much time we will spend here together.

No, thank you.

Okay, then let's get started. Did you know the victim personally?

One of the stupidest questions I had heard in my lousy life was asked. It sounded routine as if he was just asking me about an old friend of the family out of politeness. Questions asked hundreds or even thousands of times a year must eventually become routine and no longer impress anyone. At this point, I realized that I'm not a person for him, and just like the rest of his "clients" I am a number entered into the tables full of statistics. It was another quarter of an hour separating him from returning to his warm house, where his ideal family was waiting for him. His family probably looked like those whose images are placed in frames in photography shops with the passing people encouraged to buy them. The fact of being an insignificant number among a million others was evidenced by the aforementioned condition of the chair on which I sat and its varnish, which was clearly worn, marking the seat with a black streak.

The tone of the interrogation didn't bother me a bit, because I have always preferred this type of behavior in case of forced interpersonal contact when everyone knows that they would rather be away from the other and only courtesy or professional duties don't allow them to immediately leave and return to more interesting activities.

Yes, I have known him for several weeks, although I wouldn't call them nice. I killed him with a kitchen knife in the stairwell not more than two days ago, which you already know very well, so we can finish this whole thing. You have an eyewitness who pointed me out, and now also my personal and conscious confession,

I disclosed it short and simple, not wanting any further explanations and psychological games that would soften me, and which I had expected from the very beginning.

I preferred to experience all the events of the last days only internally, as well as almost everything from my earliest childhood. Only there could no one hurt me, no one except myself, which unfortunately happened quite often, much more than I would have liked.

Burdened by other people's expectations of me, from all sides, I was always trying to achieve even more than I had expected. I fell into a vicious circle from which I could not break free. Nothing brought me satisfaction or relief. There was always a new, almost impossible goal on the horizon, which I had chosen for myself. I did not make these efforts for the praise of teachers, family, or splendor. I just wanted everyone to leave me alone when I had achieved enough that I would not have to do anything afterward. Of course, that never happened, only the standards rose with each successive accomplishment.

During cold nights, hidden under the covers, unable to fall asleep for a long time, I would dream about my future home, in which I would finally feel safe and no one would have the right to judge me anymore. I was always avoiding judgments like the plague. I constantly dreamed of a brick wall of at least two meters that would separate my future home and a peaceful garden from the unpleasantness of the outside world, from all the smart aunts, various officials, and intrusive interviewers – literally from everyone. I was so stressed out going outside that I craved my own private universe. I wanted a universe in which only those I would choose could be a part of it. There would be those whom I could trust immensely and be sure that they wouldn't hurt me or turn away in a moment of weakness. It wasn't about power, maybe just about power to control myself. It was all about the break out from the overwhelming anthill, which surrounded me and was still piling up, filling more and more densely, causing stuffiness and imposing on me who I should be.

However, deep down, I knew that I would never be able to achieve true, unfettered freedom – not because of the lack of willpower, but because of my financial condition. I would often see the guilt in myself and my inability to adjust to the rules of society. At a time when most of the people around me dreamed of a promotion, and even saw the meaning of life at work, I only dreamed of escaping from the rest of society. The need to go to work continued to systematically destroy these visions of boundless privacy. This process would happen even in the smallest studio apartment consisting only of a toilet and a small room with a kitchen and an air mattress on the floor.

"Life will verify you." This phrase of my mother's echoed in my head. It was a response to any disagreement in my family home. I must have heard it a million times, but each time it gave me the same sense of incomprehension and resistance that I had deep within myself. Once again, it seems as if the thoughts have gone too far from the heart of the matter. Where have we finished?

I am sorry, but I cannot close the case with only the facts I know now. Unless you refuse to testify, which I strongly advise against. What is your decision?

Let's continue,

I agreed, seeing no better alternatives.

I understand that during these few weeks that you may have been in contact with the victim, there have been circumstances in which you had the opportunity to get to know the deceased better,

he tried to be precise like clockwork.

Of course, I knew this bastard. I even knew him like the back of my hand, even though we did not spend much time together. Rather me and him, because any combination of him with me apart of this matter, even grammatical, disgusts me. I knew him like no one else.

So, he was no stranger to you,

he summed up and wrote a short note on the new sheet of paper directly in front of him.

How can a person just murder a complete stranger? After all, murder is probably the most intimate activity imaginable. To kill an unfaithful wife or even a hated neighbor, I can understand, especially when they get under your skin with their daily dirty tricks, which are the final straws. However, I don't understand how you can kill a stranger in cold blood, you would have to be evil by nature. I believe that there are only a few people capable of it, even among criminals. I could not believe it at all. It is pure idiocy reproduced by crime fiction and mass culture. I have to admit that I didn't express my thoughts aloud. People by nature do not like to hear inconvenient statements, even if they are true.

When did you first hear about the victim or meet him in person?

he moved to the next question on the list, which he recited relentlessly from memory.

How was it exactly? I tried to remember because the excess of impressions began to overwhelm me and distract me more and more effectively despite the previous peace. The facts reminded me more or less, though temporarily they were like fragmentary images seen through a fog. It is strange, it was so recently, and yet it feels like forever. One by one, from the beginning, so as not to get confused in the rush of emotions that the memory of that fatal day arouses in me to this day.

My daughter, Milena met this soulless scumbag on a Friday night dancing at the student club of the Polytechnic University. It was probably at the beginning of December or the very end of November this year,

I finally remembered.

Did anything catch your daughter's attention?

As far as I know, he did not have any strong characteristics. His face, at first, seemed to resemble every other face of a stranger she had met accidentally in the street. Nothing special or worth remembering. It was not clear whether his eyes were green or just gray. It was certain, however, that they were staring at her incessantly, although at first, they did not arouse much suspicion with all the rhythmic swaying and twirling in circles, pairs, and alone.

You talk about it as if you were there yourself.

Nothing like that, I just heard stories from my daughter whom I have great contact with. You know, not every teenager locks up in their room for days,

I explained, losing all my urge to tell the stories in detail.

I would like to believe that there is still hope for young people.

He did not go further, so I kept to myself everything that seemed irrelevant to the case, although, of course, Milena had told me much, much more.

What was next? Loud speeches and toasts heralded endless fun and blissful carelessness. Fashionable jackets and dresses fluttered left and right despite the lack of draft. Time passed innocently to the accompaniment of music and glasses clicking from time to time. More and more often, champagne found its way to the throats hungry for fun and to the dance floor red-hot from the incessant dancing. Due to her inherent politeness and modesty, Milena returned home without any problems and in great spirits before midnight. Escorted by her two childhood friends, Anna and Cathy, she safely crossed the threshold of our flat. I knew these girls almost from the cradle and I knew that they were decent company for my daughter, so I had nothing to fear. After saying hello to me and giving me a short account of the evening, she went straight to her room to give her tired calves a rest. Milena had forgotten all about the man she had met that evening(as long as he could be called a "man" at all), and there was no sign that it would ever change. She told me about the first impression he made on her in detail later when she had the opportunity to do so. As it soon turned out, it was not necessary to wait too long for it.

Barely a week later, maybe even not that long, he began to wander around shamelessly here and there. He pretended that it was an accident that he was walking past her university and even under our kitchen window. I was pretty sure that he was looking directly at our window as if he knew exactly where our flat was, even though he had not even exchanged a word with Milena. She found him in the park, in the store, and on the way to her friends. "Coincidence," this was what he told her, masking everything with a broad smile of his cracked lips.

I was not stupid and blind enough to believe a single word of him. Unfortunately, she, my Angel, believed in all the lies he fed her and she paid more and more attention and interest to him. There was something mysterious about him that must have intrigued many girls my daughter's age. I would call him the "aggrieved philosopher" type, I hope I make myself clear enough. Over time, he changed "coincidence" into "destiny," which caused flushing on the face of such a delicate and sensitive person, with no similar experiences and thus no prejudices. Already a few days after the first conversation, she was tempted by the small gifts she found at the door and the reassurances of his sincere affection. Romantic letters, sketches, and poems, what an absurdity, but to my displeasure, the tactic he chose seemed to initially result in a delicate interest, though not yet an infatuation on her part.

Why should she not believe him? She did not know anything about life yet. What is more, she had no idea about the meanness that was happening all the time. Maybe it was a mistake that I was trying to protect her from all that dirty things and moral decay. She had no way of working out her immunity to widespread foulness. Meanwhile, that disgusting Man went further and further into his insolence, here he rubbed against her thigh as if by accident, and there he whispered his devilish charms to her beautiful innocent ears. Before I knew it, she was already maneuvered like a puppet in a theater for children who, unknowingly, admired the whole world, as if it came from a fairy tale without noticing its dark sides. I allowed it all out of love for her, I was afraid I would lose her otherwise. I was hoping that nothing inappropriate would happen and that this lousy person would go away as soon as he appeared. I believed that Milena would come to her senses in time and she would make a good decision on her own. But I was stupid, stupid and naive, although I had not suspected it before. Drip drip, drip drip.

What was the motive for your crime?

he asked again in a calm voice, as if completely unmoved that he was talking about a murder. It seemed that he treated this interrogation on the same level as small talk about the weather or sports.

Does there always have to be a motive?

Indeed, there is always a motive.

I still cannot understand why an educated Man, a father in his prime, did something like that, openly, during the day, without fear of any consequences – this time he delved and wanted to know all the details that made me commit the known act. He was like a judgmental angel, which was to decide about my body, but not about my soul because he did not receive such power and, though in his pride, he could never gain it.

A Man with apparent power only, thanks to his uniform and badge, wanted to know everything about me, and I did not want to say anything more. And all for what? I do not need these reflections on my conscience, all these games and performances. I did not want sympathy or, what is worse, compassion. Compassion exists for aggrieved beings, those who get lost in the vastness of the universe and Wander alone, longing for a renewed sense of coexistence with others – it is not for me. Why are the same questions always asked?

"What was your motive? Why did you do that?"

Still just why and why. Blah, blah, blah. It irritated me mercilessly. It must be a penance for past sins, a generational curse, or simply tormenting to satisfy one's conscience. As if the facts alone were insufficient to quickly pass a final judgment. This strange inquisitiveness and curiosity of other people always creeps in, wanting to make others like themselves, and to justify even the worst filthiness, to make people more humane despite known and indisputable facts. Their metaphysical fear of emptiness and the nonsense of existence force them to always give everything causality and order, even if it turns out to be sloppy and impermanent.

Why did I decide to do this? I did not say a word. They could not find anything in the world. I preferred the Sisyphean torments that were waiting for me just around the corner. There is always something around the corner, every split second, and even if it does not exist yet, we are already doomed to it. It happens not because of fatalism, but because we know that it is lurking, because we create it ourselves in our minds. It is irreversible, you have to accept it. You can accept it with dignity and stoic calmness, or you can poison yourself completely and burn yourself out internally by drowning in a sea of helplessness.

We sat in silence looking at each other, the interrogator still waiting, unfazed, as if he had a feeling that my answer would eventually come voluntarily. He would probably have waited even longer, but suddenly a buzzing fly appeared above our heads, breaking the silence between us. It was a hideous, noisy beast, albeit innocent. It stubbornly kept flying in new circles. In its stubbornness, it still circled and circled as if it wished to create mocking and blasphemous halos over our tormented heads. It had no right to break in here. After all, everything in this vague room had been carefully sealed. They did this so that even the smallest thought could not slip away from here and contaminate some innocent child's mind, which was to remain in its blissful and innocent unawareness until the end of its days. It was the best option for everyone, even though I believed it deep down. This fly must have lurked here earlier, waiting patiently, especially for this occasion, awakening from an eternal sleep only to mock us, baptize us and reconcile us in its primal abomination. The insect ceremony was repeated cyclically and did not allow even the slightest degree of attention to be focused on the actual reason for our meeting. The wings flapped louder and louder, which, though impossible, seemed to take the form of a deliberate provocation and a mockery of all professed values.

My companion in beastliness couldn't withstand the constant attack on his sanctity, purity, law, and order. No instructions or regulations were provided for a similar situation. The crisis deepened more and more. The constitution turned out to be completely helpless. Unable to find any other solution, he took to his clean, well-groomed hand the sheet of paper that had previously rested on the table and mercilessly he crushed his tormentor, this eulogist of impurity and corruption. The fly's dirty blood ran down the snow-white paper in a stream. The Little beast achieved its goal, its sacrifice was not in vain. At the moment its plan was clearly visible. The new executioner understood what he had just done in angry exultation and he became afraid of himself. He felt contempt for himself for having voluntarily associated himself with the dirt. He lost his coveted innocence forever, in such an insignificant and shallow way, in the way most carefree children do.

For reasons not fully known to me, I decided to deceptively use the moment of his doubt and strengthen him in his newly adopted attitude. Though I am now unsure of the rightness of this action, back then it was a kind of ambition and fun cause for me that seemed more and more tempting by the second. I was unable to resist this sudden temptation that overwhelmed me. I began to undermine, step by step, his faith in the order he had served so loyally and without hesitation for, it seems, over thirty years of his life. I started with suggestive glances, but the words spring up from my heart. Which side should I choose to attack? What will affect him and will stick in his mind? Whether anything can reach him at all? I must emphasize that my game was not intended to cause him any harm or use him, but only to make him a conscious man. To be honest, this was not a morally questionable act, and I still do not intend to change my opinion on this subject. The time had come for the first, rather cautious, attack.

Why, for example, such a soldier can legally kill and slaughter hundreds of enemies and poor people with a smile on his face and a sense of due service to the motherland and patriotism, and I could not kill one with impunity? This Man who was more of an enemy to me than the unknown soldier on the other side of the barricade who trembles in panic with the fear of dying in a war he had been forced into and which he would never have voluntarily gone to. Is the order of a general sending others to murder mindlessly or be killed higher than God's law? Whether the epaulet on the shoulder gives the right to indulgence and absolution? Should I die for the motherland? There are so many of these motherlands on the map, each beloved by its people. Should not the moral law be the same for all individuals, regardless of their position and belonging to a specific class?

I was fully aware of the mass of truisms with which I had filled my lengthy monologue, which even seemed too pathetic to me, but at the same time, I knew that I had chosen the right tactic that would strike him at the most sensitive point of his soul and stir up the uncertainty he was so diligently hiding deep in for many years.

Hearing these words, he became sad and completely silent. His face showed reflection. He knew the answer to all of my questions, but he would not admit it to himself. In the end, he was ashamed, not of having human blood on his hands, but because of the greater right to kill without any consequences. This thought must have become too overwhelming for him, but it was evident that despite his efforts, he could not abandon it. His tone changed from indifferent to compassionate. I must admit that this surprised me as I expected denial rather than reflection.

Don't you have any dreams?

Please forgive me, but that is rather irrelevant at the moment.

Tell me why you did it, maybe there is still enough time to make at least some of these dreams come true. I can't believe it all happened for no reason at all. You don't look like a bad person. I think that if we had met under different circumstances, I would probably have thought that you are someone nice,

he went back to the previous tactic, but this time he tried to catch me with nostalgia and his humanity. I was not quite sure what I should think about all the kindness he suddenly began to show. I suspected that it was not a calculation, and it resulted perhaps more from the naivety of the uniformed man. At first glance, this behavior also seemed to be an attempt to redeem the guilt he felt after killing a fly.

Thank you for your kind words, but I don't have anything else to add. You know all the technical details, it is enough.

Are you sure?

Indeed, it would be better to end our conversation already. Please forgive me but it has made me exhausted and you will probably need some rest too.

And what about the dreams he asked about? Indeed, I used to have a lot of big dreams but I didn't share my story with the interrogator. From early childhood, I wanted to become an astronaut and travel through spaces that had never been explored before without fear. Even my beloved dachshund was called Laika, it occupied my head so much, obsessively, but what to expect from a child, even the brightest one of all peers. I dreamed that I and Laika would set off on this long and inert journey to nowhere. I pictured a shiny hull, red flickering buttons, and a countdown from the speakers. The destination was irrelevant. I dreamed that our faces would appear on posters of all children. I dreamed that they would recognize us as friends. I have never desired heroism or fame; I have never become so vain. I just wanted closeness and understanding, if not family, then at least peers. However, I grew up and realized that even more unexplored spaces lie elsewhere – they are in ourselves. We keep walking forward only to fill the void that lies dormant in us, even for a moment. This void lurks ominously to expand like an infinite universe and mercilessly consumes us completely in the least expected moment. As you can guess, I did not manage to become an astronaut, and Laika made her journey alone a few years later, due to her advanced age.

From that moment on, I didn't dream about anything anymore, I was over it. Instead of resting in a steel can traversing the cosmic abyss, I was to be given time to traverse the galaxies without moving from one place to another. They already wanted to ensure this for me in their morality and goodness. I decided to keep silent and not move, even if they were to bully me, which at least theoretically was not within their competence. My companion didn't seem to be angry at all.

Instead of anger, there were more attempts to grab at least a bit of my soul. These attempts became more and more burdensome for me.

At least say it for your wife or family, completely missed, apart from Milena, I had no one left. It was for her that I got up every day, I got up after all Falls, no matter how painful they were. It was for her that I tried to be human, not just a substitute for it, a burnt-out shell with a void inside.

My wife left me years ago, it's even hard to say exactly when it happened. I stopped counting the years a long time ago, because in the initial period, it did not allow me to function normally, and someone had to take care of Milena and show full responsibility. Being responsible beyond measure allowed me to mature faster, although I'm well aware that this doesn't always work. So, I started trying to fulfill both roles, father and mother at the same time. It wasn't easy, but in the end, after many attempts and probably many mistakes, I started to deal with it somehow, although it was not for me to judge the results. The most important thing is to learn from mistakes, preferably from other people's mistakes, and I have experienced countless of these in my life. Their list could be printed on more than one encyclopedia, volumes from A to Z, completely occupying the sagging, yellowed shelf in the old man's apartment.

Playing house (although I hope I provided one for my Angel for real), arranging hairstyles, brewing tea in filigree cups, mending worn dresses, and hours of confiding in feelings. It had never happened to me before and we were learning how to open up to another person at the same time. I have always been proud of Milena and I have always tried to understand her, for which she repaid me with kindness. She has never disappointed me a lot.

The more I focused on the past, the more I realized the existence of a scene that I managed to suppress from memory after many attempts. This scene came to me suddenly and stuck in my head as if it were alive and not far away as if it had only happened yesterday.

My wife, although I'm sorry to say so about her now, only slightly smiled when she was leaving. Maybe she wanted to show her superiority, which, however, was quite pretentious. This smile, like my mother's Laugh, haunted me for years afterward, almost every night after falling asleep, still as clear as that damn day. After all these years of relationship, engagement, and marriage, I didn't deserve even a single sincere tear or a word of explanation. Almost my whole world was in ruins at one moment and the sacredness I worshiped was trampled like a smelly cigarette on the pavement with the overwhelming accompaniment of silence. And that Smile, the Smile of the machine. Motionless, stiff, and forced Smile. It was like painted on an empty, tin toy from the previous era, which can only impress with its appearance, but it is cold and unpleasant to the touch.

She felt cornered, overwhelmed by the fact that I loved her sincerely, that she was the whole world to me. It was hurting her. The disgust for my sensitivity had burned her within, as allegedly holy water burns people who are possessed. At first, she struggled with it, then she didn't want to lift a finger to save it, save us. I remained faithful despite all the pain I faced. And that last smile of hers, that damned Smile. Until now, I still feel phantom pain after it.

I know perfectly well what made her so – the reason was that lousy hospital, that rotten mortuary, full of fear and despair. I still feel disgusted when I think about that place.

According to her family tradition, she became a nurse. From her childhood, she was zealously encouraged to do so by her mother, with whom I could never find any common ground. Of course, I never openly admitted my prejudices so as not to lead to a conflict. Everyone with even an iota of a brain is aware of how work these cold robots covered with a human dome which are called nurses. Constant contact with death can affect the psyche in two ways. In the first case, a person becomes too sensitive, even oversensitive, and gives their whole self to others, forgetting about themself and losing themself at work. In the second case, which in my opinion is much more common, one gets rid of all feelings to be able to live the next day with full psychological comfort and self-satisfaction. The second case, of course, results in treating patients and others like objects, justified by the inability to focus on all those who need it. Many times, I have heard first-hand stories of those who act as altruists, and when no one sees, they mock others while chewing on another bite of chocolate cake, received as a bribe. I have heard of those who believe in no sanctity except money and their convenience but never admit it publicly. I have heard of those who laugh at their patients, always assign them hypochondria, and treat those in critical condition as if they were already dead because of the lack of a chance to cure them. "Vegetable," I won't count how many times I have heard this term spoken as something ordinary, as if it meant only a plant that lies on a shelf for too long and withers.

Case number two, an "altruist" without any feelings – maybe a beautiful, but empty dome. This is what she became in less time than expected. Meanwhile, I didn't expect it at all. I was not prepared for it. When in Rome, we'll do as the Romans do. The change took place after several months of staying in this environment and was comfortable for her. The nurses' station taught her everything. Gradually she became indifferent to everything. You could say that she had been dehumanized. This could be read especially from the facial expressions which adopted a limited range of reflexes, excluding from the repertoire the unnecessary ones. She began to act as if she had gotten a heart atrophy because of that disgusting place, or maybe she had only masked her true nature before. It spilled over into every aspect of her life, as well as our relationship. I tried unsuccessfully to fight it for several years. Indeed, for a few years, I couldn't come to terms with it. I justified her in various ways and even tried to deny what was clear as day. I invented newer and newer ways to get her out of this state. Romantic gestures, sincere compliments, Support, and attempts to understand her, everything worked unilaterally and was welcomed as long as she could benefit from it. I explained her lack of reciprocity and justified it with the way of upbringing that prevailed in her family home. Since childhood, she has been observing the relationships (though this is a wrong word) between her barents[2] who were forever in different rooms of the same house.

I tried to teach her a different life, and at first, I thought it was getting good results. It worked until the first obligations

---

[2]Parents upside down

and difficulties appeared. Then there was the pregnancy, a big surprise, which I was glad of as the greatest miracle sent from heaven, although again it seemed to me that it made only me happy. My wife went to work almost until the birth, not because of responsibility, but because of a choice that I could not understand. It became a frequent cause of our arguments. I was worried if everything would be successful and the labor would take place properly – luckily it happened. After about three weeks, she returned to work, and due to the fact that I could work from home, I stayed with little Milena.

My ex-wife didn't seem to pay much attention to our daughter, as if she was an obstacle that would be better forgotten. She began to treat me the same, although it was not easy before. She was particularly irritated by Milena's night crying, prompting her to sleep in the living room. No talk, no touch, free time with her eyes chained to the screen – it became an everyday reality. My requests for time together didn't work, and after a few months of my struggle for a family, she disappeared from our lives forever. I've only seen her a few times since then, at divorce cases, and then only from a distance, by chance, and even then, she pretended not to recognize me. Fortunately, during the first years of Milena's life, I found a way to combine work with caring for her. After that, I wasn't so lucky anymore.

How did I manage to survive, being the sole breadwinner of the family? Until now, I couldn't believe it, when I mention those times which seem like a story I may have heard from a stranger. My daughter didn't go to kindergarten yet, and as you know, a small child needs a lot of time for attention, practically the whole day from dawn to sunset, so normal work couldn't be taken into account. Begging has always been a disgust for me, and I couldn't even imagine practicing something similar, so I had to find a different solution. I walked with a pram from one place to another, asking about any possibility of earning money. Almost all of the offers required eight to *screw you* hours away from home, which I couldn't afford. All that was left was the cottage industry, which took place at night, taking care to be quiet enough so as not to wake up my baby sleeping right behind the wall. No, I wasn't assembling the pens as it probably comes to mind of many people who are just reading these memories. Instead, I made home decorations of various kinds, although I'm far from being plastic, despite all the ambitions I had in myself. It was also far from good money. I was learning two times less than people who made the same crafts but sat on a stool in a factory. However, I had no choice but to agree to this offer. It resulted in living from salary to salary and every evening calculations, just to remain on the surface, to survive one more day. I didn't want to regret anything for my daughter. Milk, diapers, and baby soups were indispensable in any way. So, it had to hit me, and there was nothing to dream about alimony – it was an "amicable" condition, a deal that gave me full custody of my daughter, avoiding dramatic scenes in court. So far, I didn't regret the decision one bit. Processed foods, repeated sticking of cracked, leasing soles, worn pants, sleepless nights - I don't know how much these factors shortened my future life. What I know is that they shortened them less than the stress I would have if I had not divorced and stayed in that toxic relationship.

The only entertainment, apart from playing with my daughter, were two books a month, bought in an antiquarian bookshop which is now located in a different place. The problem was when I bought an uninteresting book, I would then read the previous one a second time instead just to keep my mind occupied for a quarter of an hour a day. Nevertheless, I appreciate that I was able to spend at least those few coins so as not to go crazy. The end of the month, when it was really hard, I used to call it the Great Depression. Back then, more than once, to try to improve my mood, I consoled myself that I was still not forced to sneak into the basement to hunt for a rat for our stew. You would often hear urban legends about similar incidents in the eastern agglomerations, and probably some of them were true.

It was all the more true what happened during the interrogation, although I couldn't believe it for a long time.

From behind the door of the interrogation room, in our gloomy solitude, we suddenly heard despairing screams interrupted by sobbing and heavy, spasmodic breathing, as if during an anxiety neurosis attack. These screams were deceptively similar to their twin sisters in the cold hospital rooms, but here they could at least count on someone to listen and try to understand them. The desperate sounding voices I heard, though distorted due to the almost soundproof door, I would have recognized anywhere. For the first time since my capture, I couldn't control myself. My legs trembled and my stomach was gripped by an invisible hand that twisted it over and over again. The whole world ceased to exist for me in this unreal moment. It was impossible, it couldn't be. How did she get here, and by what miracle? I wished it would turn out to be just a freak of my weary mind, a sad hallucination caused by my state of anxiety. A salty tear rolled down my cheek, I could no longer hide what I was experiencing inside.

Unfortunately, I couldn't be wrong, it was Milena, my only, beloved daughter. I must have lost my mind to the end, or maybe I was dying and my mind was haunted by what had always been the most precious to me. But no, it was true, although it didn't bring me even the slightest relief. I preferred that she would have forgotten about me than that she had to experience it all over again and remember a second time what was meant to remain a secret taken to the grave forever.

The disturbing sounds also reached the ears of the accompanying uniformed man, who stood up suddenly ready for any confrontation, as long as he didn't have to spend at least one more moment with me and be exposed to the emptiness and doubts that would gradually engulf him. This he couldn't afford at any cost, wanting to remain the same person he was when he expected me. He fought fiercely for his soul just as I fought for mine, even if it was forever cursed and impossible to recover with any strength, regret, or penance.

He got up from his chair, trying to hide his haste, and headed for the door that was located directly behind me.

Whether he wanted to or not, he had to pass me up close. Instinctively I turned my head toward him, but he tried not to look at me. From the expression on his face, I read the relief as if every moment without me could become his salvation or a long-awaited rest. I felt like I was experiencing déjà vu. Do they all feel like children in the fog, crowded in this group of seemingly brave people? He left the room, leaving me exposed to all my thoughts, which swirled more and more with each passing moment.

I was left alone with this absolute which overwhelmed me more and more. At this moment, when nothing depended directly on me and I was completely powerless, a great fear struck me, and some invisible noose was tightening more and more around my neck. Anything could happen, and that terrified me. A certain tragedy is better than an illusory hope. By the way, there was no question of hope. If only I could find some certainty in this mediocre life, something without variables and unknowns. Maybe then I would be able to build something permanent. Maybe then I would be soothed for a moment, but it's impossible in a world ruled by man. It was the first time since I can't even remember when I felt totally ashamed. I was ashamed of being like them – fake, created by expectations, crammed into social roles, with no possibility of escaping from them. So, He began to dominate me. He sowed the seed of doubt in me that could destroy me or burn me out. I didn't even consider giving up, I couldn't afford it, and that would be my end. He couldn't even suppose that everything He had heard about my case so far was only an innocent prelude. I prayed He wouldn't hear anything more because it was too late to change anything anyway. The miracle wouldn't happen.

It seems that Milena told him everything down to the last detail, which hurt me all the more. She crossed the line of shame for me, most people wouldn't even be able to describe such things. Although she turned out to be braver than me, I regretted that it had happened at all. I'd rather spend the rest of my life locked up than expose her to similar confessions, which could tear all the wounds that would not heal anyway, even for the rest of her life. My poor daughter, why did this have to happen to her? I asked myself this question all the time, I couldn't get over it, and I didn't even try. They talked to her in detail, and time seemed to drag on forever. The screams had died down, but I could still hear some commotions from behind the wall, some general stir, although my ears could barely register the individual colors of the voice.

A companion in my misery returned after a minute, an hour, or an eternity. He quickly slammed the door behind him and I didn't even have enough time to see my daughter's face. The uniformed Man couldn't stand still and nervously walked around the small space between the cluttered table and the wall. In a fit of unfocused anger, he clenched his fists and opened them after a while, as if he couldn't decide on anything concrete. You could see real indignation in him. I even envied him because I was no longer capable of such ecstasy.

The rape had to be reported immediately to the relevant law enforcement authorities,

he brazenly blamed me as if it could undo what had happened, and divert the flow of a bloody river. I didn't expect him to be outraged like this by the whole incident. Before that, I had expected rather a complete dispassion. The world itself, not me, finally convinced him of its injustice. After a moment of struggling with himself, he finally calmed down and managed to stop thinking about all his beloved laws and regulations for a few seconds. If I wasn't completely consumed by worries about Milena, I would probably look at him more favorably, seeing this sudden change, his real, human face. But the worries prevailed, I didn't even answer him, I didn't have the strength for it.

Once he knew it all and rested a little bit, I saw sincere sadness in his eyes with the dark circles under them. Maybe even some understanding flashed in them. There was something else about them, though it was barely discernible. Yes, I think I saw admiration in them, or maybe I just wanted to see it because of my vanity. I couldn't count on a medal for my achievements, after all, I wasn't wearing the uniform. I straightened up proudly, knowing that I had done the right thing, although it didn't give me any satisfaction. At the same moment, he began to slouch, unable to refuse me the right. He bent lower and lower towards the document folder lying on the table as if he wanted to read something from it or hide behind it for a moment. He couldn't even take his eyes off it. It was closed and it remained so until the end of our meeting. I wasn't interested in what was inside, for him, it probably didn't matter at all. He gently opened his mouth a few times, but couldn't bring himself to say anything. I waited in silence, which was even more painful for him.

I understand,

he dared to admit it.

There is the motive that I was looking for. It will certainly be considered an affect, a spontaneous act on the spur of the moment, and you will face a smaller penalty than I originally assumed. To be honest, I would like them to not convict you at all, but the law is the law,

he tried to comfort me, even though it was completely impossible.

What can I say? I strongly deny all of these and other insinuations. It wasn't any affect. Nothing like it, even in the slightest. I didn't do it all at the moment of my first anger or blinded by hatred, but it was a necessity and a cold calculation. Time won't turn back. I had enough time to plan it all down to the last detail, logically and rationally. I would do it again today. At this point, I just wanted him to stop feeling sorry for me and look for more excuses, I couldn't bear his stupidity at any cost. I hadn't even had time to answer, and yet he continued.

Are you planning an escape?

he asked me in a depressed voice, our eyes met for the first time since the very beginning of the interrogation.

You don't have to worry about it,

I answered truthfully. Besides, I didn't know what good would it do, but I knew that the emptiness would probably never leave me again. As unbelievable as it may sound, I saw this void as something that might help me survive. Recognizing the nonsense, you can hide in it and ignore the next blows that will appear along the way.

Are you sure?

Of course.

Excellent, because someone accidentally left the door open and it would be enough to leave through it, so that we wouldn't meet again. Goodbye or Rather good luck,

he replied, which I cannot believe so far, and he left the room himself, turning off the light.

It sounded like bad dialogue from a movie in which the protagonist always avoids misfortune at the last minute. Happy endings, sloppy tearjerkers, tons of snacks under the cinema seats – I knew it too well to believe it. I didn't even hear his footsteps as he walked away as if he were just a ghost that vanished into thin air.

I sensed it was just a trick, I couldn't shake my suspicions. How could a Man of great determination, with a pre-determined worldview and mass of experiences, change to such an extent in just a few hours? From bland to extreme through just one event and that is because of a complete stranger. Would you risk your position or reputation for someone you don't know? Did he believe that he could save me in this way? This whole situation absolutely couldn't be true, or maybe I had the paranoia buried deeply in my genes. Even if it wasn't a matter of genes, my mother had instilled it in me through all the years of her training.

I opened the door despite the contradictions and fears tormenting me. Slowly I tilted my head as if it was to keep myself from being detected and I looked around trying to see whoever was around the corner. My suspicions didn't come true. There wasn't any trap and no one was waiting for me. The corridor was empty, except for the sadness and seriousness, which must have always lingered there and penetrated a person through all his pores to soak him whole, cell by cell. They wouldn't deign to miss me either.

Where is Milena, is she safe at home? This question tormented me. I was scared about her, as probably never before, though I cannot say that I have never been worried about her safety until now. Did someone even escort her to our staircase at such a late hour? I wanted so badly that she would sleep well in her Bed without thinking about all that had happened. Tightly wrapped in the lovely duet with her duvet, as she used to, from the feet to the very top of her chin, regardless of the season or temperature, dreaming innocent dreams. Reality is the worst nightmare that one can imagine.

Deprived of my previous confidence, I stepped through the doorstep left open by the would-be executioner of my soul when he decided to become a savior. Was it a victory or just a further wading into terrifying nothingness? I didn't know it at all and didn't even dare to guess. The anxiety didn't leave me alone for a moment. It was probably late at night, probably well after 3AM, but I had no way of checking it. The watch was taken from me during a body search and deposited immediately. It would be of little use anyway because it hadn't been working for years when I got it. I realized that another difficulty awaited me, I had to leave my grandfather's memento forever, which made me all the more depressed, although it seemed impossible before.

I remembered the old nights filled with insomnia, but then I was surrounded by only familiar objects to which I knew my way by heart, which gave me a sense of psychological comfort. I have already forgotten what it feels like. I entered in the dark, the judgment on me lasting for hours.

Even temporarily regained freedom didn't make me glad, it only gave me illusory hope, hope that has always tormented me. It forced me to fight again, for which I thought I had no strength left. I only had one wish – to be able to finally see her and protect her from whatever I could. I wanted to be able to hear her innocent, sweet voice again and know that I have someone to live for. I wanted to know that she is safe, even when the world has little to do with dreams or beauty.

My dearest child. She's my only happiness in this valley of tears. I immediately needed any directions that would show me how to get to her. My poor Angel. To this day, I feel disgust when I think about what happened to her, and I think about it almost constantly. I just can't stop. If I regretted anything at the moment, it was only the fact that I couldn't get justice a second time. The death of this monster was an act of grace on my part. It was a favor for humanity, but also for Him. He deserved something far worse than death. I was stupid, I could have let Him groan in pain and constantly relive what He had done to others. Salt sprinkled slowly on the open wounds would still be nothing, just innocent fun in the face of what He had done. Could I still call myself human without hesitation? Maybe what I did was the most human of all. Justice died a long time ago; it was gradually lost to politics until it completely disappeared among the applause of the public and activists of all kinds. It is hard to imagine that honorary duels were the order of the day until only a hundred years ago. Honor died too, hailed as unnecessary pride, and the world turned upside down in the name of progress.

What could help? I closed my eyes to try to calm down, to think about something I know so that I can focus better on finding Milena. Under the lids, an image of the typewriter that once stood dusty in my family home materialized. I think it was a black Remington, sent by my uncle in Argentina who never returned home. It stood forgotten in an oak wardrobe to torment my father from time to time and remind him about his unfilled dreams and ambitions. One day, feeling frustrated and regretful, he got rid of it, because it had already become an archaic trinket. Today, such machines are worth a small fortune. People can stare at them for hours, even though they threw them away earlier in the name of the progress brought by the digital era. This happens with almost everything. Probably, if my late-remembered parents hadn't thrown anything away, I would have been able to make a living from the antique trade today. People constantly try to change something, only to be satisfied with nostalgia after a while. New places, new people, new relationships, but the longing for the old ones still keeps them awake at night. I realized that I was not subject to His pattern, but it didn't calm me down, so I decided to focus entirely on the present.

I had no idea which way to go to reach the exit. The sense of direction seemed to be worth nothing in the state institutions, where everything had to be extremely universal. Wall, door, chairs, wall, door, chairs. They were all the same.I could tell from my touch that it was the simplest, most ordinary pattern. The manufacturer must have been very satisfied with the result of the tender, it was pure profit with little effort. I felt like a child lost in the forest at night, except for the fact that there was no leaf in that tangle of wood.

There were no markings on the walls, and even if they were there, I would not have been able to see them in the darkness that evenly enveloped everything around me. So much research on genetics, acting like God, medical interventions in literally all parts of the body, and yet man still remains imperfect and mortal.

A cat, a common alley cat hundreds of years ago, wouldn't have such problems as me. I don't know why the cat came to my mind, after all, I never liked them. I always associated these beasts with death for unknown reasons. Maybe at His point, I was subconsciously predicting it. Yes, I expected it to come the same day, with no pity for me.

Without even considering the possibility of an incident such as wandering around the police station at night, I didn't try to remember any details of the surroundings beforehand, for which I could pay severely. I might never meet Milena again; it would be the worst punishment for me. I couldn't let that happen. Subconsciously, I realized that I didn't have much time to waste, so I felt in the dark in unfamiliar spaces.

I had finally gotten my longed-for space travel from my childhood. You have to be careful what you wish for, because one day it may come true at the least appropriate moment. I couldn't feel the cold of the metal cockpit around me. I do remember the unpleasant touch of cheap, slippery paint on the fingertips and the Sharp corners of the walls that appeared unexpectedly under them. They forced me to take further decisions that could determine my whole future. I was constantly accompanied by the gentle rustle of a hand sliding over the surface of the walls, which might have betrayed me, but almost immediately it turned out to be inevitable if I wanted to get anywhere in one piece. Taking care not to trip over any chair, bench, or other piece of furniture, I trudged farther and farther, turning into successive winding corridors of the maze. One small mistake could have exposed me. So far, I managed to avoid them somehow, but I had a feeling that the stumble was only a matter of time. Each corridor seemed to be deceptively similar to the previous ones, and I was again a small, shabby crumb mixed in a huge pulp. I was alone again, pinned on all sides, rushing blindly. I wasn't sure if I was walking around and instead of regaining my freedom, I would only suffer humiliation.

Front page of a tabloid: *The fugitive of the year, not only did he return, but he also clapped himself in irons and locked himself in a cell so as not to cause unnecessary trouble to others. That's what real gentlemen do.*

After a few minutes, my eyes slowly began to adjust to the darkness. It didn't prevent me from fitting my tibia and crashing into the water dispenser. Fortunately, due to the heavy weight of the installation, it didn't make much noise and I wasn't detected this time. My knees became weak, they buckled beneath me, but I still didn't stop in my almost frantic march. Gradually, more and more shapes and colors were reaching me, but still no clues. The famous thread method came to my mind, but I had no intention of going back to square one. Besides, I was a terrible Minotaur myself. I wanted a change, but it was still the same sequence. Wall, door, chairs. Wall, door, chairs. Sometimes something like this damned water dispenser.

What I had feared from the very beginning of the road followed – weariness and drowsiness overcame me, and my eyelids began to slowly droop. I felt under the influence of hypnosis, which I always considered to be a scam, as were fortune-telling and crystal balls. Is this really over and I'll end up on the floor? Will I Wake up on it or will they put me in a black bag right away? Shivers ran through my shaky body, allowing me to regain a little consciousness. It seemed to me that it was terribly cold, as is often the case with extreme exhaustion of the body.

Finally, I found myself in the illuminated part of the building, although I was not entirely sure if it should be taken as a good omen. Most of all, I was trying not to get paranoid. What could have exposed me immediately would be acting like someone guilty, although a stroll around the police station at night must have aroused strong suspicions itself. Camouflage, that's what I needed – the uniform would be the best option. But where to get it? There must have been a cloakroom or laundry room nearby, maybe even more than one uniform hung loose on a chair. I could probably get one, even my size, but there was one thing holding me back – my conscience.

He killed a man in cold blood and he couldn't steal a few rags. It's comic but true, and most importantly of all - logical. In the first case, there was a clear reason, in the second one it would be just convenience. Morality has always been more important to me than comfort. I guess that's why I ended up this way. Who raised me like that? I guess it was my dad, despite everything, I was still grateful to him for it. It was thanks to this upbringing that I could calmly look in the mirror every day and not spit on it with disgust. I still had nothing to reproach myself with.

Now and then I passed silent figures that were walking in concentration somewhere. They ignored me, totally absorbed in their own affairs. They always appeared alone, walking with their heads bowed like penitents. I could never clearly see their faces, tightly wrapped in the shadow cast by their official hats. Suddenly I had doubts, maybe it was the same person that I had passed many times. That thought terrified me. Initially, I tried not to draw attention to myself, but over time I felt a growing temptation to risk and face the unknown without any logical reason, although it might have lost me. In my helplessness, I made only an act of mockery. As the figure passed me one more time, I nodded my head as if to say hello to it. Nothing happened, the gesture was not reciprocated or even noticed, and I have not tried anything similar. In my mind, I scolded myself for my stupidity and recklessness. Because of this idiotic bravado, I might never see Milena again. It was high time to get smart and stop tilting at windmills, I had lived almost half a century after all, and sometimes I still felt like a child.

I continued my walk, even more carefully than before. Panic snobs, groans, and screams could be Heard from the cracks in some door gaps. In the other rooms, there was silence and depressive emptiness. I felt like I was walking through Dante's circles of hell. I just didn't have my own Virgil to show me the way or provide at least a semblance of security. I had wandered for so long that the first stray rays of the Sun began to pierce through the windows. Despite all the beauty they brought to the world, I cursed them secretly. I was sure that at any moment I would be captured.

In an act of desperation, with a bit of luck, I found a break room myself and a policeman sleeping on duty, who decided to hide there. There was no free uniform in sight, and I had completely given up on this idea. Probably most of the employees knew each other or even knew each other by sight, and I could not play well enough to deceive someone by pretending that I'm a fresh recruit. Instead of it, I had an even more absurd idea. After some hesitation, I decided to summon a temporary deserter from the dreamland. I tried to Wake him up with a little nudge on his arm, which was flaccid and almost reached the floor. I could see no other solution. The nudge didn't work, and the navy-blue shirt continued to wave rhythmically on his once-in-a-while floating chest. If not for this fact, one might think that he had died while on duty, of boredom or old age, which would be confirmed by the turbulent sea of his wrinkles. He had a white and red cardboard sticking out of his stuffed pocket. This cardboard was well known from shop windows at a time when their advertising was not yet legally prohibited. It was only possible to read the gloomy "kills", the end of the warning slogan that was supposed to discourage you from buying. I didn't wake the old man until the fourth time, which must have made him angry. Despite the nap, he lacked vigor, so it ended up only with an unpleasant grimace.

I'm sorry to disturb you, but could you please show me the way out?

I tried to sound as natural as possible.

He did it without a Word with only a slight disgust on his face. He simply pointed his finger in the right direction and waited for me to leave so that he could return to the longed-for nap, from which he had not yet woken up well. He probably wanted to remain in this state until his retirement.

I followed the indicated direction where I finally saw a pair of doors unlike any other. Maybe they led to salvation, maybe to purgatory, or maybe they were just a trap waiting for human greed. I had to check it, I had nothing to lose.

I pushed their wings with all the strength I had left, and they barely moved. However, I did manage to slip through the small door gap.

I went outside and felt an invisible trickle behind me as if it was supposed to reveal to where I ran. It was a trickle of what I had lost, a trickle of myself. Drip drip, drip drip, again the funeral march. An endless string of cars Pierce the snow-covered street, flooded with a morning mist. Damp, icy air mixed with exhaust fumes delicately stabbed the lungs tired of running away, as if even it wanted to punish me for the fact of my existence. I tried to hail a cab, but none stopped. Everyone stubbornly rushed in their own direction. Everyone was in a hurry somewhere, regardless of the rest of the world. In a sudden panic, I started asking for help for the first time in my life, begging random people and waving my hands desperately at passing cars. I couldn't break through the noise of passersbys, the clamor of the city, and the deafening squeak of horns. Clouds of steam left my nostrils pointlessly. No one seems to take me seriously. They probably thought that I was drunk or insane. It was quite understandable; at that moment I was not sure myself if it was true. I felt completely intoxicated with the smell of exhaust fumes, the colors of the street lights, and something I couldn't define myself. It even seemed to me that there was a faint taste of gasoline on the tip of my tongue, but that was impossible and ridiculous. How would I know what gasoline tastes like? I never had it in my mouth, and yet I was absolutely sure it was it.

I walked unsteadily for a few steps, slowly trudging through the mixture of blackened snow, mud, and salt that mercilessly covered the legs of everyone I encountered. I bumped into unfamiliar shoulders and torsos that appeared in my way. The insults reached me like a blur. I remember a few images – large-brimmed hat, cigarette stench, crumpled blue dress peeking out from under the catch of a black wool coat, flickering. Under the torrent of impressions, I fell on the cold asphalt covered with the hard ice. Semi-conscious of the pain, slowly drifting away into the unknown, I passed out.

PART TWO

CONFESSORUM

THE ASYLUM

I survived, which was quite a surprise for me. Slowly, flashes of conscience hit me, and I immediately regretted it. It hurt, it hurt so bad. My head was pounding as if someone had been pitting me cyclically with a blunt instrument. I was wondering if I had had some surgery. Despite tightly closed eyes, I felt the slow spinning of everything around me, just like in a state of intoxication or during a sea voyage in an old brig. I was under the overwhelming feeling that I was going to throw up at any moment. Until then, I had refrained from doing it as much as I could. My mouth was dry and my limbs were trembling like an alcoholic going through withdrawal.

Delirium tremens follows the day after complete foulness. I have often seen it in other compatriots and it's a shame to admit, but I secretly despised them. No, I didn't want to help them at all. I always turned my head so as not to see, just not to hear. *Let them feel what they deserve with their stupidity, it won't happen to me.*

Pulsating, burning pain pierced my temples. My nerves jangled and the invisible noose tightened mercilessly around my throat again. In a fit of desperation, I was ready to beg for mercy, but I stopped myself at the last moment, as it dawned on me that it would make no sense. Besides, I couldn't utter a single word, all desperate attempts failed.

Was I finally being punished for all my sins, for the pride that I had hidden in myself? My pride was a wall for me, protecting me from everything and everyone. It seems to me that subconsciously I always expected that an undefined punishment would finally hit me and I even felt as if I fully deserved it, but I pushed my sense of guilt away and tried to forget about it. At the moment, however, it was probably something else – some undefined, unknown "persecutor," who had been dozing for a long time in order to wake up at the most inappropriate moment and spoil everything. All paranoid people know this well – fear of the unknown, fear of the fear itself, which immediately knocks you down, creating a vicious circle that you cannot break out of, which tightens more and more and sucks out all hope for a better tomorrow.

Certainly, I wasn't lying on the pavement anymore, it was far too warm and soft for that, although the surface on which I was lying was still uncomfortable. Is everything going to end well? However, something was wrong. There was a catch, as usual, a small print at the bottom of the contract, or some other hidden trick prepared by someone who brazenly rubbed his hands together. My aching spine was gradually sagging into a dense, uneven mass. In some places, it was as hard as rock and in other places, it appeared to be bottomless. I was still lying completely distracted and didn't know what to catch on to, how to get out of this lethargy, or where to seek help.

For the first time in several years, I decided to give myself a break, just a little idle time to rest. I decided to stop biting off more than I could chew. Someday one has to finally come to terms with their life, whatever it may be. It would be a really strange experience if it ever worked. I'm just not used to having free time – it even caused me some kind of anxiety. I couldn't relax even a Little, and I felt even tenser. I abandoned any attempts to rest in favor of further uncontrolled racing thoughts.

Probably a few more minutes passed and because of the stress I was now fully awake, but some mysterious force prevented me from lifting my heavy eyelids. They were as if stuck together with solidified wax or some other sticky goo of unknown origin, which caused me great disgust at the very thought of it. Was it the disgusting goo, fear of punishment, or maybe just shame? Again, probably none of the above – so what exactly? I was tired of this guesswork, this eternal analysis that served nothing in particular. The certainty about the reality of the moment vanished completely, and I felt empty again. I was still lying idle and waiting for nothing, or rather I felt that nothing was waiting for me anymore. The rebellious youth fell into oblivion and lay for good somewhere between the pages of the old photo album. I felt hypnotized.

The only pendulum I heard was the one that was permanently attached to a clock that must have been measuring the time between me and my humiliation and ridicule. I had no idea if any tormentor was nearby, and although there was no reason to think so, I was sure that something bad was going to happen to me. I could never fall asleep near any damn clock; that day it was probably for the first time in my entire life, which only made me realize how tired I felt already because of it all. I was so tired of this sick joke of the last months of my life.

For as long as I can remember, clocks have always driven me crazy, and each tick seemed louder and louder, drilling deeper into the mind of the mortal. I was able to fight it for hours, putting my patience to the test to finally lose and in my nervousness stop the mechanism of these inconspicuous machines of torture that remind us of the constant passing and what will never come back, and all that we miss so much. In my pockets, I could almost always find batteries torn straight from their guts, they were the trophies in my eternal struggle for peace

However, the time had come to push the memories away and finally focus on what was important here and now. The time had come to collect the remnants of the forces that have scattered in unknown directions and to do everything possible not to regret all the inactivity and the next missed opportunities of which there were so many.

Wait, it's impossible. I felt an unpleasantly damp pillow under my head which made my whole body stiffen by surprise. It was certainly not the pillow I used to wake up on every morning. This one was too flattened as if more than one person had used it before me. Someone must have brought me here without my knowledge, unconscious and apparently, I was in a cold sweat during my nightmares. I wondered if I had been saying something in my sleep...

if I was speaking nonsense such as sometimes happens in similar situations. Maybe I had unconsciously disclosed everything and that had been meticulously noted and stamped with the official seal to plunge me irretrievably. The place where I was probably locked up in was an even bigger mystery to me. I should be able to resolve this one issue immediately, but for some unknown reason, I still delayed opening my eyes. The curtain of the eyelids gave the impression of detachment from space-time. How afraid I was to leave this comfortable non-existence and confront what was inevitable

I felt a metallic taste on my chapped lips, which probably rubbed the pillow. I shuddered countless times – it was certainly not sweat, was it blood? Was it my own blood or someone else's? Same thing again, it will never stop haunting me. This taste cannot be confused with any other taste, even children know it.

It crossed my mind that this time I was really dying, that this was the end. I was afraid that I would never be able to change or fix anything again. I was afraid that I would never look into Milena's eyes again, and everyone except her would forget about me and no trace of me would be left in this valley of tears. Only a marble slab would remain, over which at first my Angel would cry alone, and then finally come to terms with my death and start living on. This gloomy vision aroused my internal opposition although so far it seemed to me that I wasn't afraid of death. Maybe I wasn't really afraid of death, but only of how Milena would deal with it. I wasn't sure if I was deceiving myself to justify myself in my own eyes as if fear was not something completely human and inherent in life. After all, only fools fear nothing.

I still didn't dare to open my eyes, preferring to delude myself that I still had time for it. Instead, I checked my hands for bandages or even a catheter that would be any confirmation of my condition, but I felt nothing unusual. There wasn't a single swelling or change in my body. I could have assumed that nothing more serious had happened to me, but the blood haunted me.

At that moment I only wanted silence, to lie alone as in a coffin, not to be disturbed anymore, but as if out of spite, someone began to whisper straight into my ear in a voice somewhere familiar. Someone was whispering about the knife... that particular knife that I would never forget. He knew literally everything. He knew every little detail of my actions. I'm not able to quote the exact words He spoke at the very beginning, because everything seemed to blend together and was not spoken chronologically. The sentences stopped abruptly without any logical sense, and yet the statement was perfectly clear and understandable to me.

So, this was the final judgment, the scales of weight scrupulously measuring all the pros and cons for my salvation or damnation. It went without conquest, war, and famine. Three horsemen had gone astray and only death remained. He always comes on time, regardless of merit or fault. I also decided to face Him, although I Rather couldn't count on a gentleman chess game for my continued existence. I sat down in the game with one move to check mate and I was looking for a miracle that could save me. Everything indicated that I was struggling for nothing.

It's under the pillow, just take a look,

the icy voice sounded even quieter, more ominous than before, and vanished after a moment as if it had never existed.

With yet another excitement of adrenaline rush, I opened my eyes and sprang to my feet. I was ready for the last Fight, even if I turned out to be the pathetic Don Quixote fighting against windmills. There was no one else in the empty, snow-white room, which amazed me. Until now, I hadn't believed in similar revelations, and the first thing that occurred to me was that I was in the initial stage of schizophrenia. However, I realized that just knowing the irrationality of the delusion precluded my suspicion of a possible illness, or so I thought.

I made sure the pillow was indeed smeared with blood, and it was impossible to read anything specific. It would have been easier – a message, a code, or even a sign that could give me the power to act that I needed so badly. The only thing that surprised me was that the blood had still not solidified, and I didn't feel like it was dripping from My head or any other limb. My lips weren't bitten or cracked either. I wanted to surprise myself with my fantastic intellect like a detective in crime fiction, but I wasn't able to do it. This was not in a book but a reality. Emptiness again. Well, maybe not quite an emptiness, because the stain was palpable and I couldn't pass it by completely indifferent.

They will just mock me. They will mock and laugh until they cry, pointing their fingers at me. It cannot be otherwise. I am about to pick up the pillow and see the final mockery, the nail in the coffin, which they will bury with me somewhere beyond the cemetery wall in the unholy ground among suicides and rogues. In my mind, I have already seen this inscription engraved on the marble: *Nobody is buried here, better forget about him, because he is not worthy of your attention, you enlightened and righteous people.*

After hesitating for a moment, I shook off the last layer of unconsciousness, which wasn't blissful at all. And, as announced by the mysterious voice, there was a Knife under the pillow. It was completely covered with blood, from the sharp point of the blade to the very top of the ornate hilt. It was the same knife that was the instrument of my justice. I was scared to see it, but I still had no regrets. I wanted to end this theater of the absurd as soon as possible and I reached for my shoes when I got another shock – they lacked laces.

So that's it, they still don't believe in my calculation and they justify me like a child. Everything became clear in one moment. For some reason, I felt disappointed. They always have to make everything shallow and spoil it with their overzealousness.

Who are they? They are the enlightened judges and psychologists. They are the mothers and fathers. They are the educators and old ladies squeezing and pulling one's cheeks with delight. Enough, stop, leave me alone. I felt an unpleasant powerlessness overwhelm me. Deprived of any sense of heroism, I felt resigned and I curled up on the bed in a fetal position. Maybe that was their tactic – to make me feel like a little insignificant fool who had just done something stupid and harmless.

I lay there for a while longer, but I wasn't allowed to rest for too long. Soon there would be a loud but slow knock on the door as if someone was being overly careful not to scare me or throw me off balance. They probably thought I was one of those unpredictable madmen, who can only be suspected of uncontrollable rage and running amok without much reason – one that can only be approached with extreme, polite or violent behavior.

So, this really is the end of the Fight and it's so lame. They could at least spare me all these humiliations and just send me to jail or let me die there on the street when I was free. I was aware that they would immediately lead me out of the room, voluntarily or by force, to make a laughing-stock, treat me like an underdeveloped child, and stroke my head with fear that I would not bite anyone at the least expected moment. I was expecting a packet of flavored tissues in their hands, with which they intended to wipe the foam off my twisted mouth when the door opened a little and a hooked nose peeked out from behind the door frame. Prescription glasses rested on its tip. After a moment the rest of the gaunt face joined the nose, but it didn't turn to look at me.

Please get dressed and let me know when everything is ready,

I barely heard a not-very loud command.

Moved by my self-preservation instinct, I tucked the bloody pillow and the tool of crime under the sheets, and with my hands still trembling with exhaustion, I smoothed them over as much as possible. A tool of crime? What crime?

In this case, it was rather justice and even grace as I mentioned before.

On the rotten green metal cabinet next to the bed was a crumpled, gray, diamond-patterned hospital pajamas that never went out of hospital fashion. I realized that so far, I had only been in my underwear. I was surprised that I hadn't noticed it before. I wondered how many days I had la in here. One thing was for sure, no one brought my personal belongings, or at least no one gave them to me – the drawers of the cabinet had been left completely empty.

This time, I decided not to put up any resistance as I didn't see a single way of escape. Without a moment's delay, I started to put on top and pants, so as not to feel embarrassed if someone decided to go inside. I must have looked comical in too short legs that didn't even reach my ankles, although the shirt turned out to be just right for my posture. When I was fully ready, the door swung open, creating an unpleasant, chilling draft mixed with the smell of sterility. This smell reminded me more of a dentist's office than a public hospital. I associated public hospitals with a musty smell, they were closer to the train station than to private clinics. I realized that I didn't even have to report my readiness, as I was previously asked to do – without a word of warning, a previously met doctor who looked unhealthy himself appeared on the threshold of the door.

His left hand twitched steadily, driven by a invisible nervous tic. His complexion was as Gray and dry as if he was a longtime smoker. His hair was flecked with gray that probably had appeared prematurely due to the daily stress he was unable to deal with. Despite his Young age, which could still be seen from his face, deep furrows adorned his high forehead. He looked more like a patient of this gloomy place than someone who would be able to help others or at least tame their temperament in a crisis. Appearances, however, could be deceiving – I decided not to judge it too hastily, much less underestimate it. It could all be a cleverly crafted trick, a trap I was about to set myself into.

My new, nervous "acquaintance" in the smock stood in the doorway, leaning against the doorframe and watching me in silence. He was staring right at my face, but his gaze seemed absent and blurry. It looked as if he was ashamed or afraid to speak up first, and a bit as if he wanted to take out and light a cigarette, but he was aware that this wasn't appropriate. He was thinking hard about something, or just giving the impression that he was. The encouragement to speak was not coming from me, so after a few minutes of inactivity, he finally dared to take the first step. It is also possible that he simply remembered my existence and that is why he spoke, and not because of collected courage.

It is high time for art classes, and then you will see doctor Stanley, our best specialist,

the unfortunate man stammered out with the greatest effort as if he were extremely tired.

The clock read five o'clock, I just didn't know if it was morning or afternoon, as there were no windows in the room.

Art classes – I didn't expect that. What an absurdity. Did he know nothing? After all, they must have found the knife during the search and deliberately left it here to see what impression it would make on me. And yet nothing happened. I sensed a provocation; it's just their game and it must go on. And this coincidence of names, or maybe just another annoying trick that they wanted to play on me. I decided to change my tactics and not mention anything. I decided to pretend that I didn't know and don't remember anything myself, just play dumb. Let them think I'm insane if they have to, I'll deal with that somehow. I'll give them this satisfaction so that I can see my daughter sooner. I just don't know if I'll have the courage to look at her in this situation. What would she think of me? Her father locked up in the psychiatric ward? Maybe she already knew everything? It was good that I was not wearing a straitjacket – that humiliation I would not have endured in front of my Angel.

I followed the doctor who led me straight to an art room similar to those in primary schools. Probably the only difference were the benches that were not arranged in even rows, but formed into something like a circle. Nervously, the psychiatrist patted my back, as if trying to comfort me. However, it came out somehow inept and he quickly distanced himself and retreated into the corner to observe all gathered in the room. He looked like a class teacher who could not deal with children. The age range of the patients was astonishing, but it seemed that none of them paid more attention to it than at the family reunion. It crossed my mind that maybe they even felt like a family, locked together for months and years, spending all their days together, not counting the brief visits that probably happened from time to time. The inhabitants of this unpleasant place stood sluggishly over their sheets of paper spread on the tables and didn't know where to start. They took some painting utensils into their hands, put them back again, checked others for a while, and finally abandoned them as well. It must have been repeated cyclically every day because they showed clear signs of the weariness and boredom that penetrated them deeply.

The brightness of the walls blinded me. Sounds of nature, rainbow colors, floral ornaments, and among them a group of sick, degenerate men under constant care. So, this is where the psychopaths and degenerates got their slightly boring but still Eden. Thanks to you, socialists for all time, and therefore this is one of the reasons for all these taxes and the eternal inflation. I bow down to your equality, bow my head, and congratulate you. This is the place where the murderers can gently collapse into a stuffed pouf and admire the images of the wild animals painted on the walls, almost like a safari. This is the place where the deviants can relax to the artificial sound of the waves, playing a game of poker with a kleptomaniac over burned-out matches or buttons, depending on what the casino bank has at its disposal.

No one present came to say hi or anything else to me. Probably no one even noticed. Dull, motionless stares were fixed thoughtlessly on the desks, walls, and floor. I would be lying if I said that I didn't like it. I was fed up with all kinds of conversations and telling everything from the beginning, although I did it once, Due to the lack of better activities, wanting to focus on anything but, so that the time would pass faster.

I went to the table and took an empty seat. I chose one away from the rest of the patients who had all already decided to sit down. All the time I felt the doctor's eyesight on me. I noticed that he was sneaking glances at me and writing his observations in a pocket notebook. It convinced me that he was paying no attention to anyone else but me. I don't think this is a sign of paranoia. Every time I checked to see if he was looking at me, our eyes crossed paths for a split second, only to quickly run away from each other and pretend that it was nothing more than a coincidence. At first, I tried to calmly wait out the class, not wanting to attract anyone's attention and to remain almost invisible, but he kept scratching and scraping with his pencil. He looked on at me and scratched the graphite stylus against the notebook, which was the only audible sound in the entire room aside from the fake ocean waves. No one but me paid any attention to it. It was probably the norm that goes unnoticed after a few days. Every little movement, every deep breath – everything was recorded. I looked at the doctor on duty, smiled politely, and felt temporary wrinkles form under my eyes. I didn't quite know why I did it to myself. He didn't fail to write this down as well. I stopped smiling and the pencil continued to glide hastily among the notebook's grids.

Being at a considerable distance from the doctor, I couldn't see what he was noting about me. It was seriously starting to stress me, but I insisted that I wouldn't let the stress show, as he was probably waiting for it. Though my curiosity grew with each passing moment, I wouldn't be tempted. How much free space is left in his notebook, how many changes can he still register with his maniacal stubbornness? I wanted to check it out, even though I was aware that it could drag on forever, but I was ready for it. The doctor couldn't have known that I had prepared for years for this type of situation. Trained, one could say – this word is a much better representation of the reality of what I have gone through.

But who exactly prepared or trained me? I don't think it's hard to guess.

Like a salesman, my late mother stubbornly stuck her foot in the closing door of refusal. In case of disagreement, she repeated her theses over and over until I was bored and tormented. „*You have to do this… you can't do this… because I say so.*" I was supposed to believe her words unconditionally or lose. More often she used a procedure completely different from the previous one – she would stand staring silently, arousing uneasiness combined with an increasing irritation. It boiled inside me and my hands trembling, but I couldn't do anything about it. There was no escape or shelter from it – her gaze seemed to penetrate ominously into the most carefully hidden weaknesses and fears I had yet to deal with. It was like a dueling gunfight on the field of honor somewhere in the Wild West. The gauntlet has been thrown, let blood be shed.

"*I don't want it.*" The revolver goes to her hand.

"*I told you that I don't want it.*" In response, a deafening shot is fired from her hip level. This procedure continued until the collapse of will or a lethal offense.

A Man is dying piece by piece, atom by atom, though no change is visible. This torture lasted for months, even years, as I have already mentioned. The torturer knew no mercy or, knowing it, she despised it even more. Under the guise of caring and kindness, she stripped me of any remnants of self-confidence and self-esteem. Raised in these extremes, I built a wall around myself. I have become a fortress impregnable by mere mortals.

Although the doctor who was watching me didn't seem to be anything like the ordinary, he couldn't compete with my mother, who was a master in her chosen profession.

It's a show time,

I thought to myself slightly irritated by the overall situation in which I was stuck. With age, I think I lost the submissiveness that had always allowed me to survive, although not without suffering losses. I broke my original resolve. There was nothing left for me to do other than mockery. Despite everything, I was careful not to give any reason or excuse for a violent intervention – I didn't want to worsen my already deplorable situation. I couldn't risk postponing the meeting with Milena, which was most important to me at that moment.

The plan was simple. I took a brush from a pink plastic cup that had probably been a toothbrush tumbler in the past. The cup was full of a red liquid, perhaps some watered-down paint or other dye. Without much thought, I threw the damp brush on the floor and slowly and gently poured the liquid over the surface of the paper. As a result of my actions, the chair was decorated with a truly blood-red puddle.

Unfortunately, the paint also ran over the edges of its original target, causing a terrible mess that I hadn't planned. Seeing the exaggeration myself, I flinched and instinctively tried to cover up all the chaos I had just caused. All in vain, the paint smeared even more over the entire countertop. Giving up, I crumpled the sheet that was still dripping paint, and hurriedly stuffed the scroll into my pocket. Immediately, I felt an unpleasant dampness on the outer side of my thigh. Everything was soaking through. For the first time during my stay in class, curious and nervous glances ran over me. The doctor's pencil continued to move further and further along the pages of the notebook at an even faster pace. The doctor's face, however, remained unwavering, as if that was what he had expected from the very beginning. Once again, I regretted my recklessness, but was this not the effect I originally meant? I was sure that my contrariness would put me in the grave. Maybe there is something crazy about me? I pushed the thought away because I knew it wasn't true. They couldn't convince me of anything.

I sat down quietly to lose the attention of this omnipresent mob. I tried to listen to the sounds of the waves coming from the loudspeaker in the corner of the room. Blissful relaxation wasn't coming, and more and more patients flocked around me. They were getting closer in imperceptible ways. They came in silently and stood right next to me like shadows. One of them started lobbying, shaking, and after a while, he had a nervous attack. He was close to falling to the ground, but he regained his balance at the last moment. It seems that his demented, frightened cry deafened everyone in the room except the doctor, who had previously chosen his position in the very corner of the room as if he had expected that this could happen. Words came out at a dizzying pace from the patient's bruised, foamy mouth. No one even tried to silence or calm him down. Some people even ignored the whole incident.

It's… it's… it's Him!

he stammered in terror, staring at the shapeless stain on the tabletop. He rocked back and forth and his tear-filled eyes glowed with anger in an instant.

You killed Him!

You have all crucified Him with your dirty hands! Do you hear me? You crucified Him, you bloody filthy animals! You murdered Him with your heinous sins. Only me and doctor Stanley are innocent – he repeated similar phrases over and over, unable to calm down.

I was wondering about the other mention of this local fame, Doctor Stanley. It was as if there was a kind of cult of personality in the ward, and not only among patients. It was a shame to even listen to the chanters about the murder.

The worst murder is to hit the vodka in your stupid mug,

another madman retorted, probably only to have the final say in the discussion. He failed, however, because others immediately began to accompany him. Each subsequent daredevil had to try harder and harder to be heard in the prevailing chaos.

Holy truth!

A pack of lies!

said a pissed drunk with a wiry beetroot face!

Take it back or you'll regret it as soon as you fall asleep!

No fractions were formed. The threats had no real basis and everyone knew it. They were screaming only to scream, to vent out frustration and any negative emotions. All the words that were uttered, however, enchanted the first fanatic with the murder theory even more.

It seemed as if he was about to attack someone with his fists. Anyway, it didn't take long for that. The situation was clearly getting out of control. The fanatic grabbed the nearest patient, a teenage boy, and delivered a punch right in the cheek. Then he began to shake the boy with all his might, as if he, not me, was responsible for the whole incident that had upset him. The teenager was unable to stand up. He cried and fell to his knees, still being tugged. Finally, he hid his sore face in his plump hands. At the sight of this, something broke in the attacker as well, and after a while, they were sobbing together, but the angry gripping and tugging seemed to intensify even more.

The doctor on duty finally decided to Reach – he pulled out the syringe and grasped it confidently in his tic-free hand. Then he cautiously approached the fanatic from behind the back and plunged the needle into his gaunt arm. The plunger of the syringe moved all the way down to the bottom. After a while, the rebellious patient went limp like a puppet, began to sway on his legs, and obediently surrendered to the doctor. He stopped saying anything, as if he couldn't gather the thoughts necessary to form even the simplest sentence.

Most of the patients went back to examining my "work" and pretended to be fully engrossed in it, or maybe it was because of some new perspective. The uninterested rest sat quietly at their seats to continue with their art classes. The whole Group, however, acted as if the incident hadn't taken place, probably for fear of the possibility of receiving an identical injection. I could no longer bear this theater and mockery. I was sick at the thought of staying even a moment longer in this unpleasant ward.

Meanwhile, the attending physician led his victim out of the room without saying a word. He must have had enough of the ridiculous practices that he had to carry out with his hated patients on a daily basis.

We were left in the room completely unattended, or at least it seemed to be so. Such an opportunity might not be repeated anymore, so I quickly started exploring the area to choose a potential way out. Despite the doctor's departure, the chaos didn't return, which surprised me quite a bit, considering the earlier screams and signs of aggression. Most of the patients hadn't said a word since the unfortunate couple had gone out the door. They were absent as if daydreaming.

In the corner of the room were probably the worst cases that had long ago been written off. They were simply moved from corner to corner like old, unwanted furniture, which, however, for some reason, (perhaps subconscious sentiment,) could not be simply thrown into the trash. These patients stood completely still, like shop mannequins. In their faces I couldn't see anything human, not even the smallest detail, indicating that they had once lived outside the walls of this ward. I couldn't even see any signs of life in their eyes, they were dead.

The above-mentioned cases looked blankly as if at a distant point, although some of them faced directly at a nearby wall, from which they were only centimeters apart. Probably even waving a hand in front of their eyes wouldn't have caused the slightest reaction, even a twitch of the eyelid.

A few voices from the better-prognosticate patients only whispered about this mysterious doctor who was announced to me right after I woke up and who was still praised left and right. Doctor Stanley interested me more and more with every mention I heard, but I could never hear anything specific, nothing but general praise, nothing that would give me any idea of his character or even the appearance of this celebrity. I might as well have passed him repeatedly in the corridor and had no idea who I had just met.

After a few minutes, the threat of the injection was forgotten, and the group began to behave more freely, still without the slightest act of aggression.

Various open tubes and stationery accessories began to tumble across the floor. Some patients thoughtlessly tried to repeat my "feat" but still seemed unsatisfied with the results of their experiments. More and more of the group joined, and finally, almost everyone was involved in the activity.

I saw this as my chance in the chaos and decided to take action. On the opposite side of the room, I had glimpsed a passage that may have been the only escape route that I was fully determined to take. Running away almost all my life had gotten into my blood so much that I didn't know what else to do. All that was left to do was to continue in this rush and hope that I would finally get somewhere.

At the same time as I thought no one would stop me from evacuating anymore, an elderly, obese nurse jumped out of the duty room. Her face was red from the effort. There were pulsating veins on her forehead, which seemed to emanate from one central point to spread out in all directions on the smooth surface of her skin filled with grease paint. She was breathing heavily as if she had just run a long distance. It was obvious that she had had enough of the fuss. You could say that she didn't jump out, but rather rolled out or even spilled out of her small glass room that resembled an aquarium.

Her daily color press review had been interrupted which visibly disturbed her. It was evidently the type of a step-aunt who brought sweets just to eat them for herself when she thought that no one was watching. Probably everyone had at least one such "aunt" during their childhood. She didn't even manage to remove the curlers from her hair, and in her hand, she was holding an old, almost antique umbrella, which was probably once the property of her predecessor.

Nobody seemed surprised by such a sight, but in a few faces, I saw the terror, as if they had already known the use of this umbrella on their skin and didn't miss it at all.

The newcomer glared at the crowd. She found with her eyes the patient she must have accidentally mistaken for the Prophet (that was the name of the patient with the visions who had started the whole chaos) and began to approach him with the umbrella, holding it in front of her like a sword.

Begone, begone,

she tried to push the unfortunate Man into the corner of the room to isolate him from all the rest.Apparently, she found Him responsible for all the fuss.

The attacked patient backed away with his hands raised at face level, muttering something under his breath.No one could guess the meaning of his words, be they prayers, or curses.

This is not the Prophet,

shouted someone brave or simply stupid enough to stand alone in defense of another madman.

So, who?

she roared, surprised that someone had opposed her.

The False Prophet, that's who. The real one was injected long ago and he flew away, far away, like an Angel,

saying this, he waved his hands as if they were wings and tried hard to get away from the ground by standing on his toes.

Stop talking bullshit to me,

she was unconvinced and continued to attack her originally chosen victim, already keeping an eye on the next potential target.

I figured it was High time to evacuate. Trying to look natural, I walked around the room as if nothing had happened. I tried to reach the desired exit without causing any staff intervention. Acting naturally was probably not the best idea considering the place I was in, but the disorder in the room was now unmanageable and no one paid any attention to me.

I slowly pressed the door handle, fearing that the smallest sound may result in a return and thus, with the re-company of a tormented doctor with a vibrating hand or what's even worse, initiating the alarm by any of these crazy people. Certainly, neither they nor I. We wouldn't stand for it any longer. The door handle didn't resist, the door opened.

I realized what number of doors I had to exceed in full uncertainty in the last two days and I understood how much courage requires an escape, which is widely considered to be an act of cowardice. Meanwhile, the real Coward is idle, stuck in problems.

I slipped imperceptibly through the gap or at least I thought so at first. I slammed the door behind me, hoping that nobody would notice it. Then suddenly, a flash. Darkness again. Snap and a second flash that didn't go out this time. The light of a strong fluorescent lamp had touched my dry eyes thoroughly. For a moment I thought I was blind. Only the high-pitched voice of the nurse came to me. She began to inspect me with her overwhelming anger.

What's your surname? What are you doing here? Did you swallow the pills? Which room is yours?

she asked me one question after another, not giving me time to answer.

I don't think she even expected any answers, it was mainly about the squeaking and stunning me. I wanted to stipulate my ears so as not to listen to her anymore. Only they have such hellish voices, I would recognize them everywhere.

It seemed that the unclosed door turned out to be only a trap and I'm so gullible that they tricked me like a small child. I was fooled by temptation and from now on everything could have been worse than I was expecting it to be originally. I was sure that only a few moments would divide me from the dulling injection, which would destroy all my plans.

The nurse's screams alerted the rest of the staff, which seemed to be waiting for me there from the very beginning of the whole incident. Everything had to be arranged previously, such things don't happen by accident. I was curious whether the patients themselves also played a part in the previously learned scene, or whether one red stain could actually cause such strong reactions in them.

In one moment, two large muscular men ruthlessly jumped on me. I didn't see them before because the blinding light still didn't let me see anything. Having recovered after a few seconds, I noticed what they were going to do with me, and fear paralyzed me more and more. They pressed me to the floor with the mass of their body, and in the hands of a woman, there was an item that I didn't expect. Combining forces after a short struggle, they applied a straightjacket to my sore body. I couldn't understand why all this was meeting me. I didn't know why I deserved such a life, such humiliation. After all, they could simply choose to close me in a cell and give me a break. However, I still didn't believe in Fate. What else could they expect from me? I desperately tried to free myself like an animal trapped in a snare, but it didn't bring any results – a tight straightjacket doesn't want to loosen even for a millimeter.

The aforementioned bullies lifted me by my shoulders. They led me out of the room in a roundabout way, so that the rest of the patients wouldn't see it. They always look for sensation in every deviation from the norm and after a while, they tried to imitate it in order to kill the eternal boredom in the ward for a while.

We got you now, Weirdo,

said one of them, apparently pleased with himself.

Now our local fame will take care of you. He'll get these stupid things out of your head.

Unable to touch the floor, my feet kicked in the air. It was looking like a race on an invisible surface. They led me by force to room twenty-two, the one where I had woken up earlier. This time I was left with no leeway. I was tied with straps to the hospital bed. Nobody paid any attention to the sheets that were still there. It made me sure that it was really a game, a miserable provocation, and they were just waiting for the right moment.

I felt the blood leaving my wrists, which were starting to turn blue. The ties were way too tight. I felt sick again. I tried to convince them to loosen the crippling bondage a little, but they weren't going to listen to my complaint. They were too busy arguing about priority over the newly hired nurse. Let me not quote their conversation for the sake of respect for the mother tongue and of women.

The door swung open unannounced and I took my breath away. He entered the room. He was the same greasy rat that had caused me to be there. He was the same one I had killed with the knife that was now under the sheets, covered in blood. This time the Scoundrel was wearing a carefully pressed white smock with a badge fastened to his left pocket with a clasp.

What is going on?

I demanded immediate explanations,

I couldn't control myself and wanted to throw myself at him and strangle him with my bare hands, but the bonds prevented me from doing so. I didn't twitch a bit, though I felt it tearing me apart from the inside.

Please calm down, Mr. Stan, let's not repeat everything from the beginning once again. I thought you already better, but you see, unfortunately, I was wrong,

he replied pretending to be caring, but his eyes showed a clear mockery mixed with curiosity

You must be very tired as it usually happens after an attack, right?

What are you doing here you bastard? You know very well that you should be dead, bleeding to death on that floor, to the relief and delight of mankind.

Excuse me? Would you like to tell me something? I'm afraid you haven't felt as bad lately,

he cleverly tried to look surprised, but he was like an open book for me.

It's all just phantoms, I imagined them. Don't think I don't know about this. I've already worked you out. You don't exist at all. Get me out of here and let me out. I want to go home, or at least outside, to breathe the fresh air,

I was getting more and more nervous and preferred to be in solitary confinement than to stand it for even a minute longer.

Relax, I'm your doctor, you don't have to worry about anything. Getting out of here would be no good for you. As I mentioned, you had a typical attack and you have lost your memory. Normally, you are anxious, but trust me, we have repeated this procedure over and over again,

he tried to sow seeds of doubt in me, and unfortunately, I started to lose my confidence in anything. Everything happened as if in a dream.

He looked straight into my eyes as if he wanted to challenge me, and encouraged me to continue participating in his sick games, from which it's impossible to withdraw.

I want to get out of here immediately, you can't keep me here by force,

I screamed, knowing it would be no use, but I had to try again at least.

I want to be discharged at my own request.

Unfortunately, it is impossible. You have been here for twenty years, much longer than I have been working here, and I'm sorry to say that but you still pose a threat to both yourself and those around you. After the last incidents, I'm afraid that your case doesn't promise a quick improvement,

he announced, staring at my card on the bed, which I hadn't noticed before. He reached for it and wrote something on it so that I couldn't see what it was.

I want to see my Milena; you won't forbid me to do that. She'll explain everything, she'll take me away, I'm sure of it.

Milena? Ah, yes, you are talking about your daughter again. You have to understand that she practically doesn't know you. Anyway, I doubt that she would like to come here from abroad, we've already been through it, Mr. Stan,

he didn't give up.

Please focus and try to remember anything. You have to come to terms with reality at last. You can't run away from the truth all the time, you can't live like that.

This is ridiculous, I saw her yesterday. What should I remember? What did you do to her? Stop confusing my head at last, I'll kill you all,

I blurted out, though I had no intention of saying any of it. I immediately regretted it and noticed a barely perceptible expression of satisfaction on his face. I felt as if someone else was speaking through me. I was no longer in control of my behavior. I felt that they may have finally managed to break me. I was clearly losing this game on every field.

You can see that we can't let you out of here just like that, he emphasized with a smile.

As for your family, as far as I know, your wife left you about twenty years ago and the court granted her full custody over your little daughter. Since then, you have gradually deteriorated, more and more, month by month, and so you have come to us. Since then, no one has visited you and no one has even called you to ask about your health.

Where's Milena?

I didn't give up – I want to call her at least.

Unfortunately, we don't have her phone number, and besides, you don't see your daughter at all and you only think that you live together. Every week you tell a different version of this story and you are convinced of it. You often change her name, so at first, I'm never sure who you are talking about. Please understand that this is only an illness and we want to help you. You just have to let us do it and cooperate, and who knows, maybe you will come back to society again one day.

I will not believe a single word of yours,

I said it as if I was addressing a group of people, although I was perfectly aware as to who was behind it all.

I have evidence, you can't tell me nothing.

Only peace can help you now, stop fighting and accept reality. It is how it is. Nobody is trying to convince you of anything. After all, subconsciously, you must understand that everything I say is true and forms a logical whole that cannot be denied.

Maybe I didn't kill you, but you can't take your revenge like that, you monster, even you can't be so inhuman,

I said, though without much conviction.

Ok, let's try something different. Give me proof that you are healthy. We can make a deal. If I get even one little proof that I'm lying, I will let you out of here today, otherwise, you will calm down and allow us to help you.

No problem, I have the evidence, and it's undeniable. A pillow, it's under the pillow, a knife and blood,

I confessed, fearing that this was what he was waiting for.

I'm sure there's nothing there, please let me check,

he replied without a little hesitation as he walked over and leaned in to check the truth of my words. The knife was gone and the pillow was clean

I don't think you should have any doubts now. Now I hope that you will keep your part of the agreement. We don't need any more troubles here, we already have them beyond measure.

It was here. The knife was here an hour ago,

I explained myself like a child accused of a lie as if proving brutal acts would bring me pride in front of the victim himself. Though the word "victim" doesn't fit this Bastard at all.

I can assure you there was nothing there. Why would someone hide a knife here and then take it away? Do you see any traces of blood here?

Someone had to wash them or change the sheets,

I tried completely exhausted.

He fully ignored my last words and I had to come to terms with the fact that I had failed. His mouth corners lifted a little bit again and he turned his back to me. For a split second, I thought I saw the knife in the pocket of his apron, but I wasn't sure if it was just a delusion, which I was starting to believe more and more. I didn't have the strength to fight it anymore. The feeling of passivity completely overwhelmed me. Fortunately, he couldn't see it because he didn't deign to look at me anymore.

Now please give the patient the drugs,

he said to the two men who had been listening casually all the time, and which I had completely forgotten about, focusing all my attention on my namesake.

One of the helpers opened my jaw with force until something crunched, while the other pushed several large-sized tablets into my mouth and made sure that I swallowed them. I almost choked on them. Initially, I tried to hide at least some of them under my tongue, but it didn't work. The torturer in a single latex glove remained relentless and constantly watched over my conscientiousness. When they managed to achieve their goal, they let me go, and my teeth chatted so loudly that I was afraid of losing them. Fortunately, after a short examination with my tongue, I realized that they were all in their place. After a few seconds, I began to feel all my limbs go numb and I was losing all my willpower, which surprisingly seemed even pleasant. Having checked the tightness of my bonds, they left the room and me completely alone in my dull state.

I was lying there tightly belted and maybe I'm ashamed to admit it, but I was crying. Put simply, I was crying like a little child left unattended for a while. Hours passed and I still didn't know what was real and what was just a delusion. I stopped worrying about reality, and not feeling coherent with it. I imagined that I was talking in turns with my daughter, grandfather, and dad. Everyone I love seemed to be so far away from me, they seemed to be unattainable. Most of them were no longer present in this world for many years. I started to think about eternity, about God. I wanted Salvation. Consciousness was returning to a normal state.

I wanted to Pray. I wanted to beg to know the Truth, but at the same moment, I heard a gentle knock on the door, as if it was up to me to let someone in or not. It was an strange feeling for a man who had all his limbs shackled, to hear the knocking and not be able to do anything about it. In the rhythm of the knocking, there was calmness mixed with melancholy. It seemed that it was a necessary routine for someone, an imposed duty from which there was no escape. I didn't react.

Can I come in?

there was a soft but loud voice that I haven't heard before, or at least I couldn't remember it. There was, however, something distinctive about it, although it was difficult to tell exactly what.

Yes, you can,

I replied, though I didn'twant any visits from strangers. However, I didn't want to be rude to someone who wasn't going to hurt me. I was also curious about what this meeting might bring, as I subconsciously suspected that it wouldn't be an ordinary conversation.

Despite all my suspicions, I didn't expect what I saw. A snow-white habit dangled from the guest's emaciated body, resembling a coat hanger. The habit appeared to dissolve in the darkness. Gradually it faded and turned gray as the closing door cut off the last beams of light entering the room through a temporary gap

Good afternoon,

I greeted, surprised to see the clergyman.

Do you want to confess me?

Good evening. I'm only a Monk. I haven't been ordained a priest, so I can't do it, but I can call a chaplain if necessary.

Please don't worry, we can manage without the chaplain. Then to what do I owe this visit if not confession?

Actually, it is about confession, except it is I that came to confess my guilt. Do you deign to listen to my faults?

I confess you? I am not a priest either. I'm even further behind this than you are. I am not even an altar boy.

Yes, I want to confess to you, to another man. This is my penance imposed on me by His Excellency, the Abbot. I come here every evening and confess my sins to my neighbors.

What exactly is this repentance for? It's a little hard for me to understand. Is it for humiliation?

Indeed, yes, the humiliation, but only so as to help me. I'm to be assessed to feel guilty, to feel repentant, and to regret the sins I have committed and still commit. Guilt will help me to free myself from temptation, only then will I be absolved.

And you don't feel remorse without all of this?

Unfortunately, I can't. It would be much easier for me if I did.

Not at all?

Not at all,

he replied without hesitating, though he stared at the floor as if he felt remorse over his lack of remorse.

So why confess in a place like this?

I can count on someone to listen to me here. Patients are unlikely to complain of too much work during their days here.

Oh yes, you are probably right,

I confirmed, having nothing better to say.

I can't jeopardize the image of the Church, and you wouldn't be believed anyway. Even if you were to preach the most sacred truth, people would nod their heads with pity and smile at best. Nobody will believe the Madman. No offense.

Don't worry, I am not angry. I'm only here by accident, although probably everyone says this. What then did you do? I have never Heard of such repentance, it's almost unbelievable.

I fell in love with a woman,

he began bluntly.

In a Nun,

I interrupted him, but I found this knowledge essential.

What? Please don't even joke like this,

he seemed upset as if he thought the nuns were strange, haunted creatures, detached from all earthly affairs, perhaps even a lower caste.

I'm sorry, let's continue.

Every man locked between thick monastic walls, stuck in a small, stuffy cubicle, instinctively dreams of love and it's a shame to admit, but He also dreams of closeness... not only an emotional one. Simply put, He dreams of closeness to another body, its warmth, smoothness, smell, and moisture. He dreams about the second body ceasing to be foreign and becoming everyday life, a refuge and an escape from all the problems of this poor world. Paradoxically, in the case of finding love, the person in my position is forced to withdraw even deeper into the cold emptiness of his cell, seeking Salvation from sinful thoughts and temptations. The emptiness, however, deepens, even more, the longing for the outside world, for sensations, the so-called "real life". However, I'm not allowed to live "truthfully". This is how everything loops.

After all, Love is beautiful, God approves of Love

Indeed, but not the sensual one. I'm not allowed to Love this way.

Where is this written in the Holy Bible?

Does it matter? Even if it doesn't stand like this anywhere, I have vowed purity, and despite everything, I can't forget not only about Her interior but also about Her body, which for me is like a Miracle, proof of the Creator's perfection.

Love is a gift from God, not everyone can get it. Sensuality was also finally created for something. I would like to be able to Love again and admire someone, enjoy it, appreciate it, and thank God. Why does faith need to be sad and eternally associated with repentance? Let's stop whipping and focus on something that can be changed for the better. Or is mortification only our national trait that we must cram everywhere? Everyone is always complaining, including me, I'm fully aware of it.

Please don't lead me into temptation. The life I have chosen is a constant work on myself through self-denial, solitary contemplation, and searching in silence for the voice of the Lord who calls us to Himself.

I hear a deep sadness in your voice. You still love Her, right?

Yes, I love Her truly.

Does She know about it?

Yes, of course, She knows, I couldn't hide it, but I didn't do anything more about myself. Believe me. There are limits that mustn't be exceeded.

And how did She react to this confession?

She reacted as badly as possible... with reciprocity.

Did you decide on something together? I don't believe that it only ended with a confession and everyone went their own way.

She feels sorry for what I have vowed. After all, She understands that we shouldn't, that we can't be together. Such is human fate, ashes to ashes, dust to dust.

Isn't it a greater harm, then, to reject Her feelings, to con-demn another person to misfortune and loneliness in such a cruel world?

And what about my vow? I promised it to God

What does this vow mean today? If even the Pope can withdraw them, it means that they are essentially worthless. I think that it's enough for you to apologize to God, and He will understand everything for sure, in the end, He is merciful.

Please, don't mock God.

I'm not mocking, I'm a believer myself. I don't under-stand where these suspicions come from. Coming back to your vows, you were a youngster at that time, steeped in various utopias that fade into oblivion with age. It's absurd that at such a young age, a person can be thought to be capable of making a binding decision for life. Such ceremo-nies should only be allowed in the thirties when for most of the time, a person is fully formed and knows what he wants out of life.

Everyone would condemn me and point it out.

So, it's just about that,

I interjected, hurting his self-love first of all, but then he quickly returned to the agenda.

Maybe you are right. You don't realize what it's like when everyone just nods over and over at every sentence you say. Contrary to appearances, it's addictive. It's really hard to give it up, to be knocked off the pedestal.

I guess the old ladies...

The old ladies? Everybody does it, every single one. Even teenagers. Behind my back they say what they want, and they show off, but as soon as they stand in front of the habit, they react in the same way as to the cassock. They stutter and nod their heads thoughtlessly like those figurines of angels and shepherds who move in churches after children throw in a coin.

My guess is that it may indeed be so. Then another question is more relevant. Would you blame yourself for your actions?

There was an eloquent silence that seemed to contain the answer in itself. The monk looked up from the floor and he looked somewhere on the wall, not daring to look me straight in the eye.

No, I wouldn't blame myself because of it,

he finally said, slow and barely audible. I read his lips more than actually hearing the words.

Then I'm sorry, but I'm afraid that this is sheer convenience. You just don't want to truly sacrifice yourself for the other person,

I said to motivate him to make the right decision, but I must admit that I was afraid of his reaction.

Can you keep a secret?

He surprised me with the question that this time he asked louder. He ignored my diagnosis as if he hadn't heard it at all.

After all, you yourself said that no one would believe a Madman anyway, and even if I weren't a Madman, hardly anyone would believe it. Anyway, I don't even have anyone to talk to. You see what my situation is now.

It doesn't look good,

he admitted.

I got a portrait photo from Her, in which She Smiles so beautifully with Her head slightly tilted towards Her shoulder. There is pure joy in Her eyes in the photo, and this lousy sadness all around me. Every day before going to sleep, I look at Her. Her long, light brown hair and imagine how She smells like mint mixed with a bouquet of spring flowers. Nobody knows about this gift, otherwise, I would have to give it back. These are our rules but this photo is the most valuable thing I have, even if it is but one. Everything belongs to the order. *Dura lex sed lex*. I haven't mentioned this photo to anyone, you are the first. I keep it hidden in the Holy Bible, specifically in the Book of Job. It reminds me of how much I lost by joining the order. Fortunately, I didn't lose my faith. I love God, but I already hate those walls where I have searched so hard for Him. This is the last place where I would expect to find Him. I would sooner look for true faith on the street, among the aggrieved.

You can see that maybe it would be better to stop lying to yourself and others,

I tried again, but in a softer tone, hoping that maybe this time he would finally give me an answer.

It's easy to say that in your place. Although I must admit that the worst drama is taking place inside monastery walls, where curious pilgrims are not allowed to enter. Humans are always so lonely there that I often think that I would rather go do normal, physical work.

Really? What kind of job, would you say?

I would go to work where something is happening. I would meet different people, and talk to them as equals because so far, I feel that everyone is a stranger to me as if an invisible wall had grown between us due to the way of this life, which unfortunately I chose. I'd rather do something useful like a piece of furniture, a radio or a meal. I'd rather do something that serves another human being. I would really like to start to live, not to vegetate as I have done so far.

Have you ever worked full-time? Or better, overtime? Have you come home tired, not having the strength to even smile? Were you sleepy before the evening and sleepy in the morning? Have you been swept over and driven by idiots? Have you had a constant headache?

No, I haven't,

he admitted.

That is what "working with people" is for me, as you put it so nicely. A lot of people would give up a Fortune and even cut off an arm or a leg to have more free time. For example, I would love to spend all the mornings at home reading more and more books from an antiquarian bookstore, waiting for the return of my daughter whom I love more than my life.

I guess we always dream about what we can't have.

You can achieve it all. I would suggest, however, be more careful with these dreams. Please believe me that I'm not saying this because of jealousy. I only want to help you.

Do you really think so?

Yes, I do.

Now you want to spend more time with ordinary people, probably ready to even become a socialist or a communist; you would even despise them, forced to associate with them every day, tired of the company of people you don't even like, who irritate you mercilessly with their tiny little details.

What little details do you mean?

Well, they usually irritate with their boundless stupidity, which goes hand in hand with their unshakable belief in having a monopoly on the truth… and sometimes they just irritate with the way of pronouncing "r", the timbre of their voice, the manner of moving. Sometimes that's enough to get sick of someone.

Isn't that an exaggeration?

Once upon a time there was a stupid watercolor painter who persuaded people to murder for stupider things than today, even for the shape of the nose.

Let's not generalize.

Let's not forget.

Those were different times.

But the humans were the same. It is enough to look at what's happening today in the schools and yards,

I insisted, which displeased my interlocutor, who wanted to see good in man at all cost.

I have to go now… no, I want to go now,

he corrected himself, as if disgusted or afraid of the sin of lying.

What will happen now?

I asked out of human curiosity.

I have no idea. Probably nothing will change,

he replied resignedly

I'll probably come here again tomorrow to repeat what I do every day.

Think about it again.

I have a lot of free time to do that,

he turned around and he seemed to want to leave without saying goodbye.

Please wait just a moment,

I wanted to shout, but I said it not very loudly, as if embarrassed, and he stood still, waiting for my next words.

You can finally ask me.

What should I ask you?

he became interested and didn't even try to hide it.

You can finally ask if I forgive you your sins, after all, it was the purpose of the visit, confession.

Do you forgive these sins?

he asked doubtfully.

In the name of humanity, I forgive; in the name of God I can't, but I believe that God is more merciful than man, so there is nothing much to worry about.

Thank you,

he said, and this time he left without stopping.

Opening the door, he let the light in for a few moments. It was as if by the force of his will he had passed the gate to the Kingdom of Heaven, leaving me here all alone, the scraping of metal indicating that someone on staff had locked the door from the outside.

I lay idle for hours, tied up with straps and abandoned. I no longer knew which port of consciousness to dock into. I had advised others on what to do so many times. I had spoken with confidence as if I knew how to live and yet here the truth was quite different.

There was nothing to shape me. I hadn't experienced war unless it was a cold one. It was a cold one, as cold as everything that surrounded me. Like the house I had left. A war full of gunfire and bombing had never happened despite widespread fear that had seemed palpable in the air. There hadn't been any direct encounter with death. There wasn't any heroic struggle for the sake of a higher ideal. Even an ideal had been lacking completely, not only one for which to live but ordinary, smaller ones.

I had never been in the army because of the condition of my spine. Unable to fight – they stamped the release papers, signed them, and said goodbye. Zero experience despite my sincerest intentions. No one had time for collective trying, and the lonely trials of experiencing anything became a torment even more than the total stagnation and endless boredom of everyone else that surrounded me.

Man lives in herds by nature, and it's difficult to renounce it. I have tried to do it a million times without success. I have tried to withdraw into a private world of literature but from its pedestals, the people who wrote the words I read were as inaccessible as God looked to me. Moreover, they acted like they were gods.

The environment offered a different solution to this tragic case of mine. The solution was mechanical work and discipline. It's not a machine that imitates a human being that is the problem, but a man who has long ago become only a machine. A man only in a collective, because individuals had already died out in the last charge with the saber against the tank of the present day. Constantly working to have somewhere to sleep; to sleep in order to have the strength to work.

Enough of these shallow comparisons to a cog in a machine. Without the specific cog, the machine won't move even a millimeter. Today, each of these people are completely redundant. Now it's all just an impersonal compact human mass without any distinctive features. Everything is changeable depending on the whims. It is a conglomerate of everything that is nothing. It will no longer be a Trojan horse or a stick inserted into the spokes that will derail the established order. It can't, It lacks any ideals. Ideals can be treacherous, and as quickly as they rise to their rank, they fall and become forgotten forever.

Still, I have to live. I have to force myself to live this nightmarish life, full of everyday games and artificiality. I have to force myself to make faces and poses that the real actors themselves are ashamed of. I have to force myself to play for her, my daughter. I have to save her from this fate that befell me, the martyr of all surrounding vagueness.

Slowly, I began to reassure myself that the stay in the hospital was indeed a fresh thing for me and that everything that happened to me after waking up was only a hoax that was intended to lose me, keep me in the hospital, or take me away from my daughter for unknown reasons. After a while, however, I began to doubt It again. My head was completely confused, and It needed rest more and more.

I was falling asleep when the key turned again in the lock and someone was led into my hermitage. This time, not a single ray of light came through the door as if there was complete emptiness behind It. It was too dark for me to see the face of the lead in, but there was something familiar about His posture. I was almost convinced that I had met Him before, but I couldn't say where exactly.

He walked hunched over, scared, and shuffled his feet with resignation. The Three Newcomers were silent. Until recently, I too had wanted silence, and now it had become unpleasant, even annoying. The Man sat down obediently on the bed on the other side of the room. He took off his slippers, lay down on His back, and let Himself be strapped down like I was. It seemed that He already had quite a lot of experience undergoing this procedure, everything went much smoother than in my case, as if He was assisting the perpetrators himself.

I waited for these perpetrators to finally disappear and at the moment when I heard the characteristic sound of the lock being closed, I tried to make my time by talking to the Stranger. The loneliness had started to bother me too much and it became as unpleasant as silence.

Excuse me, Sir,

I tried to get his attention.

He didn't even answer a word. He was silent as if He was ashamed of something. It seems He even tried to turn His back on me as if He was angry with me, but the belts prevented Him from doing so. I stopped trying to make contact and regretted that they had brought Him here because it made me even more anxious than what I had originally felt. We lay there without saying a word, and the only thing that could reach my ears was the sound of His swallowing, which irritated me mercilessly. It is sometimes quite nice to be silent alone, but in two it is quite unbearable.

To my surprise, the mysterious visitor spoke up after a while of torment and made me dumbfounded. I didn't understand what He muttered, but I knew that voice, it was the voice of the treacherous scum who had hurt my daughter. By this point, I was sure that I had lost my mind or that someone was just playing me. I must admit that in the past I also often had the impression that someone had decided my Fate from above, although it seems to me that I'm not a fatalist; it must be a matter of rigorous upbringing, without being able to decide anything.

What did this dirty monk want from you?

he asked, pronouncing the word "monk" as if in deep disgust, then spat on the floor, which wasn't the easiest task while being tied to the bed.

Does it matter? Why should I tell you about this?

Because you want it yourself, you know it. You couldn't bear to keep silent, not now when you know my identity.

We talked about love,

I replied evasively, not wanting to reveal the whole truth, so as not to give him the satisfaction he certainly expected.

And you, could you love someone else? Could you really love, and not just utter empty words as it's used to do nowadays?

I always thought so,

I lied; I don't know why.

He had already figured me out, as if he was reading my mind, I had no doubts about it.

You thought so?

he picked up taunting.

So why didn't you just do it?

There was no opportunity or time for this among all the responsibilities I had had since my divorce.

Maybe you should lock yourself in a monastic cell and become an ascetic? You are bound by this pathetic monk more than you think. You are both equally deceitful and comfortable. I know what you were talking about.

How is it possible?

A good magician never reveals his secrets. This is the first and most important rule.

Who are you?

You know who I am, although you are afraid to say it out loud. You were afraid as a child, don't you remember?

I have no idea who you are, everything you say is nonsense.

You are not just lying to me. You lie to yourself, first of all. Think carefully and you will find the answer to your question.

Never mind, I don't care anymore,

I lied again.

I know you care. Remember that only with my help can you get out of there,

he gasped asthmatically as if he was about to spit his lungs out, but after a while, his voice returned to normal.

You need me as much as I need you. All you have to do is to promise me obedience, and you will be out of here in a minute, able to shut yourself up alone again in that bunker of yours from which you don't even like to stick your head out.

Shut up. I never want to hear you again. I know you don't exist. I would like to finally come home and go to sleep, sleep through it all, even if for a year or a hundred years.

Are you sure? If I don't exist, why are you talking to me? Anyway, this isn't the time for mockery and banter, the knife is still under the sheets. You can free us with it, just don't let anything stupid come to your mind.

My hands were too corrupted for me to check to see if he was telling the truth. Moreover, he was probably well aware of it from the very beginning, as he smirked, not hiding it too much, as soon as I tried. To my surprise, I realized that I could clearly see his face as well as the rest of his body. I wasn't sure if my eyes had gotten used to the dark, or if the reason was completely different but I hoped it was about the eyes.

Suddenly he broke free from his bonds. There was also the possibility that he had only pretended to be tied up by them. The second option seemed much more likely to me. He sat down on his bed and began to swing his dangling legs slowly, giving the appearance of boredom or impatience. At times, he made his face like a capricious child who craves new experiences.

There's only one way you can get rid of me,

he said as if reading my mind again, guessing my innermost desires.

You would have to get rid of yourself.

What exactly do you mean?

I asked, though I was almost sure I could guess what he might be talking about.

You know exactly. Don't pretend to be dumber than you are, although you are limited and you can't see beyond the end of your nose.

That's not true. I didn't do anything for myself. I live only for her, for my daughter, my little girl. Let me see her at last, I'm sure she hasn't forgotten me.

Oh, what an Altruist. Forever just you and you, everyone's sick of it. As for your daughter, she doesn't know you. You have imagined everything because you couldn't come to terms with that reality. Why would I be making this up? Think about it.

Maybe the knife I saw was also only an imagination?

I was hoping for the confirmation of this one hypothesis.

No, that knife exists and it's still under your sheets. I can give it to you on one condition.

What would I do, and what exactly do I need this knife for? If Milena doesn't even know me, which I don't believe in, what would I do next? It would all be pointless; I might as well be lying there.

Since you have nowhere to run, and everything turned out to be pointless, maybe you'll make it easier for everyone and you'll end your unpleasant existence now, without further adieu,

he got to what I expected from the very beginning of our conversation, yet it hit me unpleasantly and I felt seriously offended,

anyway, note that you're only thinking about yourself again. You don't care about your daughter but about being loved, and these are two different things.

Shut up, you monster, don't say another word,

I screamed, which only sped up my beating heart.

I was afraid that what he was saying might indeed be partly true. He had an incredible power of persuasion. He seemed to hypnotize me with his confidence, but I still tried to resist all his powers and charms. However, I was getting weaker by the moment.

So, you are just an ordinary coward, just as I thought, You are still stuck because you tremble with fear at any change. It's a miracle that you change your underwear at all, after all, you'd also have to make a choice.

I am afraid of almost everything, but today I'm not afraid to admit it for the first time. I'm weak and comical, and yet you are no match for me.

Come on, please, the classic self-esteem building by criticizing others.

I can kill you again,

I threatened him, realizing that I was talking nonsense and that I was completely powerless, but it didn't stop me.

I will kill you a hundred times if I have to. You're like a nasty cockroach that needs to be crushed.

Is that right, I'm like a cockroach; I'm squashed and I keep crawling on, I'll survive anything. You lack this flexibility, so of the two of us, you'll always be in the losing position.

He got out of bed and paced the room. There was no sign that he was afraid of being seen. He walked with gentleness, like a landlord in his palace, pleased by the state to which he had led me. At one point, he stopped halfway to my bed and stood like a statue, face to face. Due to his immobility, he irritated and provoked me, knowing full well that I was unable to do anything. My hands jerked towards him, but the straps held them back just like the first time.

I'm about to call the doctor, ward, police, authority, or whoever, and you'll regret this constant harassment of innocent people. For too long I've tried to deal with everything alone. For too long I've been running away from someone else's help.

I'm the authority here. I'm the Lord and the Creator. Though you've gotten a little more wise in the end, it's too late. Time has come for you,

having said this, he slowly began to make his way towards me with his hands clasped behind his back as if he was hiding something.

I was sick of it, and for the first time since I was born, I was really afraid of my life. The self-preservation instinct worked and I screamed out. I wanted them to drag him or me out of the room at all costs. Solitary confinement seemed like a fond dream, compared to spending more time in His company. The hooked-nose doctor with the trembling hand ran into the room and looked around. He seemed to be surprised.

Why are you screaming in the middle of the night? Are you mad or what?

he hissed, but after a while, he realized what he had just said, where we are, and he became confused himself.

In the meantime, the scum returned to his bed and made himself comfortable on it, crossing his legs.

Please take him out of there. He constantly persecutes me and he doesn't let me live in peace. My advice would be to lock him up in solitary confinement and to not let him go out anymore, lest he hurt anyone else anymore. He urged me to the Suicide.

Who exactly do you mean?

the doctor asked stupidly while my namesake was having his best time listening to our conversation. Nothing could spoil his mood.

Irritated, I pointed my finger at his bed without saying a word, and waited for justice to come at last. The rogue wasn't impressed in the slightest. He lay still with his legs crossed, taking absolutely no care as if my words had no meaning.

There's nobody here, Mr. Stanley,

the doctor said as he looked at me searchingly.

He's lying there, I can see him clearly as you are here.

I assure you there is no one there. Please try to sleep.

The scum was laughing with the best of my despair. For one moment he calmed down. Then he got up and walked over to the doctor, standing right next to his trembling hand.

He grabbed his hand gently and held it down, trying to keep it still. After a while, however, he got bored and let it twitch freely again. The doctor still didn't react, as if indeed everything I saw was only a prediction, a product of a sick mind that needed to be kept locked up.

Give him an injection,

the rogue suddenly turned imperiously to the doctor, who this time clearly heard it and didn't even pretend otherwise. He leaned over me, and I felt an icy, trembling hand tighten around my wrist. The needle came out from nowhere and slipped into me imperceptibly, making me sleepy and blissfully unaware again. All I could hear from behind the falling curtain of my eyelids was His unbridled laugh.

Who should I be? Who am I now? Who?

All the contradictions that met me exposed me to more and more torment with each successive beat of my knocking heart, or just some dilapidated and long-forgotten machine, which was supposed to serve some time for some unknown purpose. I was tired. I decided to give up and not to fight anymore.

PART THREE

PARADISUS

HOME FOR CHRISTMAS

The alarm clock pulled me out of the drowsiness, though it was not easy for it. I realized it was an alarm clock that I knew all too well. It was my longtime "companion" that had annoyed me consistently every morning, Monday through Friday. Of course, it was an electronic alarm clock, because as I mentioned, I hate ticking and I can't get used to it for anything in the world. Praise the technology, praise the integrated circuits. My hand hit the elongated plastic button and the room fell into silence again.

I had to make sure that this time I was not dreaming anymore and that I was lying on my bed, because after all these impressions it was hard to believe anything, even my greatest certainty, the familiar aroma of pine furniture reaching my nostrils. After many years only I recognized this aroma; for others, it was weathered, being a sufficient confirmation of deliverance. Finally, I was able to breathe a sigh of relief. A tear of happiness escaped from under my still-closed, slightly quivering eyelid, and my breathing slowed and became even.

For the first time in a long time, I felt blissful, even though I had never been tormented by such paralyzing visions as this nightmarish one. The state of carelessness has been with me recently, probably during my school days, or rather during the summer holidays, when most days I wasn't forced into any unwanted company or duties.

I was able to open my eyes and not be afraid of what might happen to me around the corner. There were no longer any suspicious freaks, no whispering phantoms, no pain, or even just annoyances. When I opened my eyes, the sight of my bedroom had never before given me so much joy as at this particular moment. How much satisfaction can be given by an ordinary routine? To have a little corner watched millions of times, which can still delight in the same way, even though it has no right to surprise anyone with new details.

So, I indulged in my little, everyday ritual, to which I never paid much attention to, namely, as I did every morning, I tore off a page of a daily calendar that was hanging right next to the bed. I didn't have to get up to reach it. My hand automatically moved in the right direction to grasp the tiny sheet to tear it off, the warmth of the duvet warming my legs pleasantly. I crumpled the soup recipe on the back of the page. Then I looked at what was going to be waiting for me, as it announced its next page. I must admit that I didn't expect what I saw. I felt pleasantly surprised, not to say delighted.

In a large, red font, reserved only for special days, there was the inscription "Christmas Eve", the time of waiting for the Saviour, a time of Joy among loved ones. I immediately thought about my Little daughter, who had always loved the whole Christmas atmosphere and had been waiting for it all year round. She waited for Christmas more than for her birthday, counting down the number of days remaining until Christmas. I admit that I too liked Christmas, all the trivial matters that tormented me daily were on that day sidetracked, and only what was important mattered; no one was able to spoil it. We were a microscopic, loving family who appreciated each other's company.

Suddenly, I was disturbed by the telephone on the bedside table on the other side of the bed. It rang for the first time since time immemorial, and I had even forgotten about its existence. It's strange that so far I haven't decided to liquidate it and free myself from its small but still monthly bills. In a year, something could be put aside.

Slowly and suspiciously, I looked at the dark green handset from which a coiled cable cord stretched half a meter. Nowadays, similar examples of this archaic technology can be found in museums of technology or in other retirees' apartments, which could have also been converted into open-air museums with a clear conscience and validated at the entrance. After a moment's hesitation about answering, I picked up the handset and put it to my ear.

Hello? Hello, who's calling?

I tried to find out, and my curiosity grew with every moment like that of a child. I expected Christmas wishes or even an interesting mistake that would stimulate my imagination.

Silence.

I waited.

The silence continued.

I was going to hang up, but something prevented me from doing so. I held on tightly, my grip deathly, until my hands were sweating. Maybe something was still going to happen.

Nothing happened.

I was in limbo.

I realized that I wasn't the only one in this; after all, the person on the other end of the line hadn't hung up either, and was listening to me. We both were sitting there in silence, me and Her or me and Him. It doesn't matter. We were separated by a distance of several meters, several blocks, or several hundred kilometers. Though I had believed the opposite, I had no right to know who was calling, and I had no right to be naïve enough to believe that someone would answer my question. The times of calling the switchboard were over forever. I sat there hypnotized and, surprisingly, a sense of understanding came to me. Maybe this is just a study of the unknown. Maybe it was a journey into space like the one that I had dreamed of in my childhood. Such a journey at your fingertips, now and here. The silence and emptiness are the same, but there's no need to be afraid.

I returned to Earth.

I hung up the phone.

It's good that nobody spoke in the end, it would have spoiled the whole of my impression.

A smile appeared on my face. Sometimes there are moments when a person is satisfied and doesn't know exactly why; this was such a moment. I got up refreshed and full of energy. I opened the door of the pine wardrobe and looked into its interior. It was a typical men's wardrobe, even a stereotypical one. It was half empty and contained the most necessary of clothes, most of which I had been wearing for several or even several dozen years. Usually, I don't pay much attention to my appearance, but this time I decided to choose something special and festive for this day. This may be considered trivial, but I partially believed that the clothes a person wears could affect that person's mood. I didn't think about the choice for long, because after a while it turned out to be obvious.

I put on the sweater Milena gave me last year to greet her and please her with this little gesture. It always brought a wonderful smile to her face that I loved and admired so much. In a second, it cleared me of all my worries and negative thoughts. I always smiled back at her, automatically.

I wanted to go to the kitchen to iron my sweater when I noticed a scrap of paper sticking out from under my bedroom door, with a note written on it. Slightly puzzled, though not fearful, I bent down to read it. I recognized the handwriting immediately.

"Dear Dad,

Today is our big day. On this occasion, I have a little surprise for you under the Christmas tree. You can open it earlier, I won't get a bit angry, because I know how much it means to you. Wait until you see what I recently found behind the wardrobe.

I'm sorry that I couldn't be home this morning and help you with all the preparations, but I promised my friends that I would spend at least some time with them today. You know what Christmas is like; it's not only a time to forgive, but also time to remember your loved ones. I'll certainly not forget about you too, dad. I promise you that. I look forward to our dinner together and our annual singing out-of-tune Christmas carols. The neighbors will have to forgive us again, but I wrote about it before.

I love you very much, Dad, and thank you for being there. I'm always proud of you,

Your Milena"

This is the law of youth. I would do the same at her age if I had such an opportunity. Despite everything, I was glad that she was happy and I was sure that she wouldn't let me down because, as I have probably mentioned many times, she never did and it wasn't going to change.

Encouraged by the letter, I put the sweater aside and headed into the living room to find out what it was my little Angel had invented this time. Under a plastic Christmas tree that still remembered Milena's early childhood, there was a box tied with a crimson ribbon. It was my daughter who taught me to feel the joy of Christmas, not because of gifts, but because of her selfless love.

I untied the ribbon, lifted the lid, and looked inside the package. It turned out to be a cardboard Matryoshka. As I reached into the bottom, breaking from the layers, my eyes saw a bundle of gray paper, which reminded me of my teenage years. I unwrapped it, listening to a rustle that hadn't been heard for so long and I was shocked. It was my beloved grandfather's watch, but the hands moved steadily, and most importantly, silently on the dial. It was the first time it had happened since time immemorial, and here I had thought it was gone for good. The tears of emotion flowed down and I didn't try to hold them back.

It touched me so much and I began to remember all the moments I could remember with my grandfather. Fortunately, there were quite a few of them. I could probably write a book about them. The flow of nostalgia pushed me to do something special. I've been thinking about various possibilities. I decided to make a small pilgrimage to the places that I remembered as unique from the times when my grandfather's room was my only refuge, when I would look at postcards of the world with him and I feel safe as if the whole world was enclosed by these four walls. In turn, I decided to give Milena a small gift because I wanted to repay her for such a wonderful gift that I had received. I turned off the Christmas tree lights before going out. I washed and returned to my pine closet in my bedroom to get dressed. Of course, I hadn't forgotten about the sweater.

To give my pilgrimage a special character, like that of my grandfather, I put on a coat and a gray cap that he used to wear in winter. I had kept it in my closet all these years. It still looked like new. I left without haste, making sure that everything was in its usual place. I turned the keys on both locks and walked down the stairs, leaning against the railing, exactly as I remember it from when my grandfather and I would walk around the neighborhood when I was a small child. A life without rush, a life for itself, the You of small gestures, that is what my grandfather taught me, and I've always dreamed about it.

I left the staircase. Outside, it was cold, though sunny and not windy. The sun's rays reflected off of several-centimeters of white fluff, which evenly covered the lawn. I stood admiring the surroundings, the steam escaping my mouth. Almost everything delighted me. I enjoyed the view of the trees, blocks of flats, and the old pavements. I began to wonder where to start my pilgrimage, and what point to set as the first because there were at least a few possibilities. I wasn't comfortable enough yet to just go in any direction and enjoy the road itself as my grandfather would have.

After a short reflection, as the first point of the pilgrimage, because of the day, I chose the annual Christmas exhibition, which was always held in the same place, organized by the same people, in the same period. Only the decorations changed according to the most recent geopolitical situation and the ideological trends prevailing at the moment. First from Soviet, through American, and now on to Chinese which imitated the Scandinavian ones, only cheaper.

I was going to the other side of the neighborhood, which was supposed to take about twenty minutes. On the way, I saw many places that still remembered my childhood. I passed local shops that had always scared people with their high prices. Their owners changed cyclically, which didn't help, as if these shops were under a mysterious curse. Next, I went through an underground passage hidden under a tram line to shorten my way and not be exposed to the sinister gaze of the hunched old women who swept the area through the windows of red wagons.

I walked past the VHS cassette rental building, which now housed a supermarket, to slalom as if on skis, between the blocks and reach the one street that was full of monumental townhouses. Most of them were inhabited by retirees, people who had achieved recent success or some in the past or were important members of the previous political system. Right next to them was a cooperative club, which was also established in those years, but adapted to the present situation. Only the name of the cooperative still brought to mind workers' movements. Instead of a crowd of workers, there was a charming white fence next to the building, which separated the garden of the restaurant, which was located inside the building. It shared the ground floor space with a modeling club for children. Next, there was a post office building, a household chemicals warehouse, two large villas with gardens, and another building of this cooperative, which resembled a trampled mushroom with a wide base.

The surrounding blocks up to the top were covered with white corrugated metal sheets, which reflected the sun's rays, especially in summer. Although they didn't blind passers-by or children playing on ladders or swings, they made this part of the district seem brighter than the rest of the courtyards, where there was a deficit of metal. It even seemed that the grass grew a little bit faster here and was greener. I was only surprised by the fact that, despite the passage of more than thirty years, the white sheet metal remained clean, or at least it seemed to be so. Nobody appeared to have washed it in all these years, except the rain, and yet it had no smudges on it, unlike the car bodies near the block.

Passing those huge steel mirrors, which didn't reflect anything but the light, I only had to pass the row of garages on Minister K. Street, the local parish, the pedestrian crossing, and finally, the street appeared, where the seasonal exhibition was located year after year, to which I was just heading.

On that street, there was a large row of street lamps, which, together with the road signs, served as targets for snowballs each winter. For a moment I felt as light as if I was only a few years old again, and the biggest problem was a scratched knee while playing or a hole in the pants pocket, through which change is notoriously falling out.

I bent down and grabbed some snow into my bare hands, and felt even more chilled. I felt that I was alive. I wanted to roll in the snow, to make a snow Angel, to pour a bucket of ice water on myself to further enhance the sensations I was experiencing. I made the snowball and threw it at a lantern. I missed and then I missed again. First, second, third, throw after throw, it was with childish joy. Initially, the pavement was empty. I wasn't embarrassed by anyone's eyes. I could just be myself. I walked down the street a few hundred meters declaring war on the lanterns just as I did when I was a little boy.

Then, more and more children started gathering in the street, but I still didn't care about it, and I could say that I was even happy.

The sound of Christmas songs heralded my proximity to the exhibition, where I soon would arrive in an excellent mood. Even before going inside, I was charmed by the flickering glow of snowflakes falling from the sky, melting on the noses and tongues of children who tried to catch them only for themselves.

I slipped in after a few people who had the same idea as me. I wonder what tempted them for this Christmas visit - memories, boredom, or last-minute shopping? Maybe all of the options at once? I didn't have the time or the courage to check it out, so I broke off from the newcomer group and headed straight for my favorite aisle, which I had been heading to right from the start. There were tables all around, covered with red and green tablecloths on which there were all kinds of snow globes. Each one contained happy microworlds, which were filled time and time again with beautiful melodies from the music boxes hidden in the bases.

This music seemed to me to be a masterpiece of composition, although my Nation used to consider only sad works as outstanding things, which were meant to provoke deeper reflection, or at least they used to pretend it. For me, the special ones were the sounds that could fill me with real peace, sounds that transferred me to a better world for a few seconds and vividly painted my memories.

I looked through all the available snow globe designs, including reindeer, snowmen, penguins, and even camels hidden under the glass. In the end, I was able to choose the only globe that concealed the stable in which the Saviour was born. I decided to buy it for Milena, it would be our annual tradition, which had almost filled one entire cabinet in the kitchen cupboard.

I had what I had come for, yet the hour was still early and I didn't have to hurry yet. The desire to warm myself prompted me to visit a few more alleys to admire the hand-paintings on blown glass baubles and to admire the aware-ness that I didn't have to hurry anywhere.

Walking through the alley with Christmas trees, one had the impression that they were tearing through the taiga, only with a concrete floor, an alley with chains resembling a fash-ion show in the pre-New Year's Eve period.

As I stood at the last booth filled with a mix of all kinds of articles, I felt that I had spent enough time there. I started to get ready to go to the cash register, which was on the oppo-site side of the exhibition. I took a few steps and suddenly I felt that someone was watching me. It was just a hunch and yet I was almost certain it was true. I must have had a similar feeling for the first… maybe for the second time in my life. I turned but no one was behind me, or at least I couldn't see Him.

In the previous, more crowded parts of the exhibition, I also didn't recognize anyone in the swirling crowd. There were only faces full of tenderness, smiles, and relaxation, like in some unreal utopia, but it was true; this is how Christmas Eve works on everyone. At least for all those who are not lonely, hungry, and cold on this day. I moved on, but sud-denly I heard the crack of breaking glass from behind me. At the very corner, behind the bookcase, there was a broken bauble. Slowly, not wanting to be noticed, I approached the site of this suspicious event and noticed that a small, ragged boy was crouched behind the bookshelf. He held its head with both hands as if he were trying to shield it in fear of the blow that could come from either side.

The boy was about eight years old and had a black right eye that was swollen as if something bad had happened on the same day. Probably more than the flashing lights, he had been attracted by the warmth. He looked at me with a fear that he tried to hide in a typical child's way. I felt sorry for him. Something about his physiognomy made him remind me of a little Christmas Angel who had lost its wings somewhere and stayed with people for good. I couldn't tell exactly what made this impression, because none of the traits, unconnected with the general, showed heavenly qualities – neither the blond crew cut nor the rather tall, though nice, forehead. A steel carabiner was attached to the boy's belt loop. It was holding a lanyard with a small bunch of keys, probably for the family home, but maybe they made me think of the boy as a potential assistant to Saint Peter.

Will you tell anyone it's me? It was an accident, I promise, he said to me in a broken voice that had yet to be mutated.

Don't worry, I'll be as silent as the grave,

I promised and blinked my eyes to cheer him up a bit, which might have looked quite funny considering the circumstances.

Thank you very much. Please don't think I'm a coward.

Don't worry, I won't think anything like that. Is there something you'd like to get this year for Christmas?

for some reason, this question came to my mind first. I hoped it wouldn't embarrass the boy.

I would like to get a black chess knight.

A black chess knight?

I was surprised

Yes, I lost it and I have all the rest, so I don't need any of the other pieces.

I was captivated by his modesty. I didn't have time to answer yet when from an unknown direction a security guard came up to us. He was about fifty years old and had a bristly mustache yellowed from tobacco.

Please forgive this little boy, I'll pay for the damage,

I tried to ease the situation and do at least one good deed that day.

Sure, you will pay, and this ragged boy will continue to wander around here, scaring the clientele. Do you hear me, you little rascal? You have to get out of here, but now, so that I won't have to see you here again.

Have some pity for him, it's freezing outside, and here he's able to warm up for a moment. After all, he's not hurting anyone.

If you are so smart, take him home or even adopt him,

he spoke harshly, feeling himself the master of the situation.

Then that's what I'm going to do,

I said and looked for the boy, but he was gone. He had seized the opportunity to escape the potential threat unnoticed, of which he was probably used to.

Please don't forget to pay for this bauble, finally, as you declared to it,

the mustache Man said as he was leaving.

I won't forget,

I assured him and went to the cash register. On the way, I looked for the boy, but I couldn't find him anywhere.

I paid for the products, and a crumpled receipt ended up in my jacket pocket and mixed with the mass of its predecessors. I keep order at home, but rarely in my pockets. Only when the clothes are to go into the washing machine, the pieces of papers piled large in the pockets, are they then put into a garbage can without a long examination.

The glass door with the Christmas company logo slid open in front of me, letting the icy breeze inside. I immediately thought of the boy who must now be out wandering the cold, alone. At the same time, I realized that I wouldn't be able to find him alone, and even if I could, it probably wouldn't change anything. It was evident that he was suffering from a kind of pride that refuses to accept help from others.

I left and wondered which way I should go. Many of the places of my childhood no longer existed in their original form, transformed into modern commercial premises and offices, and some were left with a void that no one filled anymore.

I thought about the disappearing professions or those that had already disappeared forever. How many of them had there been in human history? A small watchmaker's workshop, once located under the stairs of the cooperative building, was now scaring with its walls marked with traces of peeled-off adhesive tape and a dusty table that no one wanted to take, even if for free. The booth, which used to be the shoemaker's workshop, had turned into a shop with a huge "BEER" sign; it sold mainly alcohol and lottery tickets. Addictions come in pairs.

Other stores and premises had gone bankrupt or were taken over by larger companies, which was natural and inevitable. I didn't cry for them. Maybe sometimes only the people who owned them were missed. Everything used to be more human, but I did not doubt that now it's much better and more comfortable.

In the past there were free spaces, covered with woods and undeveloped fields, now they were occupied by more and more residential estates each year, although the birth rate had decreased. We had become a society dying out in prosperity, although everyone subconsciously anticipated that the successive and subsequent social laws would be the thing that finally destroy us.

It was time to move on. I had the idea to move in the direction that the minute hand of the watch would show me. I looked at my wrist and again marveled at the beauty and simplicity of my grandfather's watch. It had a lightly worn dark brown leather strap and unmarked white circular dial. One could say – a classic of the genre without any unnec-essary design mess. After a while, I realized that the hands were resting motionless over the dial. I had completely for-gotten that it was a hand-wound watch. Time seemingly had stopped, especially for me, allowing me to continue to live in the beautiful moments that remain in my memory and not to worry about the passage of good moments that may have happened to me that day. I was so glad Milena had found this watch.

The hand of the watch was stopped halfway between four and five, which I wasn't very happy about because it heralded the abandonment of my beloved neighborhood as I was close to the border of my district. I decided, at least, to try to find something interesting there before another point of the pilgrimage came to my mind, allowing me to turn back on the right track.

I realized that I didn't have the right gift for my daughter. Dreamy visions and an excess of emotions made me completely forget about it. Hopefully, it wasn't too late to find something special and not just anything that would be available everywhere.

Excuse me, do you know what time is it?

I asked the first passerby I met.

It's exactly half-past twelve,

he replied, checking the clock on his mobile phone, which he kept at the level of his face all the time.

Thank you very much, merry Christmas,

I happily replied, having found out that I would have time to find a gift before the shops closed.

Merry Christmas,

he replied, but as if absent, never taking his eyes off the tiny screen which seemed to hypnotize him. It's a miracle that he didn't stumble over anything.

I wound up the clock on my wrist and set the time so that I wouldn't have to bother anyone with similar questions for the meantime.

I always had trouble choosing gifts for my loved ones. Everything seemed to be a bad idea or not good enough for me. Every year, the same situation happened; I would walk for hours between the shop windows or shelves, bursting at the seams with all kinds of goods, to finally give up and leave the stores empty-handed again. Usually, I ended up having to make a handmade gift myself, which took half a day and sometimes even longer. I may say immodestly that it usually turned out quite well, but over the years most of my ideas have run out, and the convention itself seemed increasingly hackneyed, even to me. Everyone knew more or less what to expect. When you have lived with someone for over twenty years, having at least two occasions a year to buy a gift, such as Christmas and birthday, the possibilities to come up with an original and satisfying gift becomes very shortened.

Fortunately, the hand of the watch, like a prophet, pointed me in the direction of a quite large-sized bookstore. It came like enlightenment to me, and it seemed like an obvious solution. I was surprised that I hadn't figured it out before.

Milena was fascinated by books, and specifically classic literature, which made this year's task that much easier for me, the more so in that almost always at dinner she told me about what she was reading, so there would be no risk of a duplicate.

I passed a large, now-deserted parking lot. Walking past the gas station, I noticed a long queue of people of all ages who probably wanted to buy alcohol to forget about problems and supposedly warm up. The next day, people like them would be found dead in the snowdrifts, and the radio broadcast's unpleasant statistics between Christmas songs and memories of famous people who had also died that year.

A short distance away was the afore-mentioned bookstore, though not of the local type, with the so-called "soul", but an ordinary chain store, which looked almost the same in every city. The amount of time left until Christmas Eve dinner, however, did not allow me to be guided by *bourgeoise* sentiments or other whims. I had to prepare everything.

I broke through two snow drifts that slid sideways, obstructing most of the path, and turned right. The book store's illuminated sign greeted me from a few hundred meters, which thoroughly cleared of snow, unlike the rest of the pavement, was covered with a thick, snow-white eiderdown. Every year, polls showed that fewer and fewer people read books, and at the same time, more and more bookstores sprang up like mushrooms after the rain.

I got there, and the automatic door slid open in front of me, revealing a large space filled with bookcases on which the cold light of LED panels shone. Everything was in its place. Everything was clean, even, and arranged in categories, in alphabetical order. Each book was displayed as it should be, but something in me, a little capricious note appearing, that I missed the mood that prevails in used bookstores, where it takes a good half an hour to find the author you are looking for, and you are never sure what you will end up with through the hunt.

I passed the gates with their sensors, the presence of which in bookstores always amazes me. I suspect that they were only dummy sensors supposed to influence potential thieves as bogeymen, and have no right to actually work. They could also just count customers coming to it; huge companies love statistics.

I headed to the appropriate section as suggested by the signs everywhere and I started browsing through the books, looking for just the right one, the only one that I knew would fascinate my daughter at least for a few dark winter evenings, when it's better not to leave the house after supper.

Excuse me, can I help you?

I was surprised by an employee who suddenly appeared to disturb my peace in a second.

Of course, I'm looking for a gift for my daughter. Do you have *The Karamazov Brothers* of Dostoyevsky?

I asked, wanting to shorten my stay in this place and return to the right pilgrimage route and the magical atmosphere that I felt until I entered this huge store.

Is it something from this year?

quite a serious question was raised that made it impossible for me to hold back my nasal giggle, despite my best efforts. Still, I didn't want to be a snob, so I quickly got it under control.

Excuse me, did I say something wrong?

I'm sorry, don't worry about it. I'll look for it myself. If you don't mind, I'd like to have a look around.

Of course,

she replied a bit embarrassed and disappeared as quickly as she had appeared.

I maneuvered alone between Balzac, Proust, and Orwell. Finally, of course, it didn't end with one book. I have already said that everything always seemed insufficient to me. I chose two books – *The Karamazov Brothers* by Dostoevsky, which I managed to find after a few moments thanks to the order on the shelf, and *The Trial* by Kafka.

To my delight, the bookstore also had a shelf with chess and all kinds of related items, such as check clocks and professional books, containing records of the finest matches played between grandmasters. While it's true that they didn't sell black knights individually, I decided to buy a replica of Kasparov's chess set. I had no idea if I would be able to meet the poor boy again, but always, if I didn't meet him and give him the one knight, I would keep it for myself as well.

When I was a kid, there was nothing in the stores but long queues. You had to wait a few hours to buy a random item and you felt like the winner of a world cup. Now there's everything you can imagine but no time to live your life. Two jobs to pay off three loans, the third job to buy some useless things you don't need at all. If you miss your past, you can always visit the special shop rack with vinyls. Why not? I did it. The majestic faces of legends looking at you. David Bowie, Iggy Pop, Mick Jagger, John Lennon and... one little dead sparrow between them. At first, I thought it was a joke, some weird toy to scare me, but its smell was too realistic. Only wild city birds smell like that. Fumes, garbage, and moisture mixed into one aroma. The bird had its wings spread as if it had just flown out of the album cover behind it. *Magical Mystery Tour* by The Beatles, remastered masterpiece in the new foil with a sticker - *Buy it and you will receive a free digital version.*

Yeah, little birdie, *all you need is love* but there's no magic, we all belong to the *Lonely Hearts Club*,

for some reason I started talking to the bird as if I was insane.

The brand-new shop rack imitates old wood and rusted steel. The vinyl albums imitate my childhood when I wasn't able to buy any of them. The icons are immortal on the covers. Only I am old and the sparrow is dead. When did it happen? I remember listening to birds singing together with my grandfather. He had a feeder on the balcony. Every winter, whole families of birds flocked there to give us a free concert, to present us real music without any corrections. This music wasn't on the shelf. The feeder was thrown away after my grandfather died; the birds have disappeared from the Stars street together with its unofficial king. Maybe this sparrow was a descendant of one of my grandpa's birds. Maybe it was the last one and now the legend is over.

Thinking that I had found everything I needed from this temple of consumerism, I went to the several-meter counter, behind which only one cashier stood that day. To my surprise, I wasn't the only customer who was buying a book on Christmas Eve, when it was normally time to prepare the traditional twelve dishes. It wasn't only me who had postponed buying a gift until the last moment, or maybe these were other lonely people who were looking for companions for their Christmas Eve dinners in the form of writers who already had left this world.

There was a girl behind the cash register who was about ten years younger than me, maybe even a little more. She looked depressed from behind the counter polished to a shine where you could see yourself. The saleswoman, despite her attitude, appeared to have something magnetic about her, something difficult to define. I felt I was staring at her longer than I should have, but on the other hand, I didn't want to stop. Thinking about how sad it must be to be at work on such a day, I decided in any way I could to try to bring her mood up, although it seemed to be a miracle that I might be able to achieve it. I didn't even know how to go about it or what trick to use. A few minutes passed, and step by step, person by person, I slowly moved forward in the queue. Finally, it was my turn to come face to face with this woman.

Good afternoon, Sir, do you have our loyalty card?

the learned formula sounded, said thoughtlessly thousands of times a day. It didn't bode well.

Good afternoon. I don't have one.

Do you want to set one up?

another regulation point was ticked off in case of possible incognito inspection, which could be expected even on Christmas Eve, and maybe even moreso on this day.

No, I don't, thank you. I'm sorry but I'm in a hurry.

Of course. Maybe a bookmark on promotion?

now we had a full set and finally, I could count on the possibility that I would see something real, human in her, though only a shadow of emotion.

Not today, thank you, but I love seeing a smile on such a nice face,

having said this, I was surprised at my courage.

I also realized that I said it loud enough that the whole queue heard my words. I felt the suspicious glances of its other members on me as if they suspected that I was trying to seduce a woman who was clearly younger than me.

Fortunately, she took it in a very positive way and smiled for the first time since I'd seen her, which immediately made me happy. I put an image of the king on the tray, who seemed to be looking sternly at me from the banknote, perhaps even admonishing me. Laura, as the badge indicated, put the king in the appropriate drawer, depriving him of any further judgment, and then bent down for a moment as if she was looking for something under the counter.

Thank you for the kind words. Here's your change,

she said, giving me two bills and a few copper coins.

Thank you again for such a beautiful smile. Merry Christmas!

I said as I left, and although I wanted to say something more, nothing meaningful came to my mind, and I began to fear the ridiculousness, the banality of it all.

Merry Christmas!

she replied with a still cheerful expression, though I noticed there was some barely perceptible tension in her, or maybe a little uncertainty. I found it rare in such a charming woman, but it made her all the more charming.

As I hid the change in my wallet, I noticed that there was a piece of paper with a telephone number written between the crumpled bills. For the first time in my life, something like this filled me with great satisfaction. It's probably vain, but I was immediately overwhelmed with a self-confidence that I often lacked in the public space, outside the walls of the fortress which was my apartment. It was nice to be attractive to someone after so many lonely years, or at least to feel like that for a moment.

Risking the anger of the people behind me and risking the ridiculousness in their eyes, I allowed myself to look at Laura one more time. She had a lovely, thin face with large green eyes giving the impression of two water-smoothed emeralds hiding behind the eyelids that stood guard over this treasure. There probably wasn't any lipstick on her thin lips. They delighted me with their perfect shape, perfectly harmonized with her pretty, slightly protruding cheekbones. Her mid-back length hair was the color of a red fox, but I saw no greed in her. Her small tattoo behind her ear looked innocent and didn't spoil her charm. It was partially covered by a double chain connector earring which gave nobility to her appearance. She was wearing a standard work uniform, but I wouldn't mistake her for anyone else in the crowd. I'd rather see her in a vintage evening dress dancing a waltz with me. Some little mysterious detail made her look like a saint. Saint Laura, not the one from Spain, by my personal one. I believed She could just cure my sorrow. I was sure that only

She could save my soul. Only She could be my redemption and salvation at once.

It's been a long time, or maybe I've never felt like this; I wanted to kiss her passionately, look in the depths of her greenish eyes until the end of the world, to put my arms around her, and never let her go again. It was all so strange, and unusual, especially since I don't believe in love or even infatuation at first sight. I didn't even know anything about her, and suddenly I wanted to know everything.

From the moment I divorced my wife, it was hard for me to believe in a love other than a parental one, and I felt that now that could change. It surprised me immensely. She was looking at me, slightly ashamed, gently pressing her lips together in innocent silence.

Excuse me, do you want to buy anything else?

I heard the voice of the woman who was standing directly behind me, which I expected from the very beginning.

No, I don't. I'm just leaving,

I replied, not wanting to arouse a sensation.

I will certainly call you,

I whispered to Laura so that no one else would hear it this time.

I hope so,

she replied, not hiding anything.

I walked away from the cash register, watched by the rest of the customers, but I didn't care about their opinion at all, and it was as if they ceased to exist for me –as if the rest of the world didn't exist anymore.

There was only one thing that worried me, but it was an important one – whether this beautiful woman would accept the fact that I have a child, an adult daughter who lives with me. Milena has always been the most important to me and I can solemnly swear that this will never change. I was afraid that even if the fact that I have a child didn't put Laura off, it was possible they wouldn't accept each other. After all, Milena was no longer the little child who needed a mother, and they were only different in ages of about ten years. I worried it would be awkward, that I was already too old to start all over again, or if I was even capable of finding enough feelings and enthusiasm to delight another person. I also worried that I might hurt her. She could have a child too since I knew absolutely nothing about her. Would I be able to accept that? After all, her child could still be underage, if it exists at all. Or maybe she is also a divorcee or a widow? My heart sped up at its work. As usual, I exaggerated everything, even if I didn't have any real information.

I realized that maybe, in fact, I was afraid that someone might hurt me, that maybe I was afraid to open up to someone again, to leave my comfort zone, to destroy a wall that I used to separate myself from the rest of society for years. It was then that I remembered a recent dream, a strange scene with a monk, how I disbelieved his logic, his paralyzing fear of change, and stagnation. I was doing the same thing at this very moment, contradicting my own advice.

I decided to try and call her the same day, as soon as I got home, and to make an appointment with her, a date. However, I needed to ask my daughter first, so as not to disappoint her. The bookstore was only supposed to be open for another three hours, so I was hoping to call her later that evening.

As I headed for the exit, I looked again at all the books that were resting on the shelves. There were thousands of them – thousands of authors, stories, experiences, millions of hours to put them on paper, all crammed into this one room in a most soulless way.

The enormity of the bookshelves that I had to pass as I walked out of the bookstore reminded me, by contrast, of the small bookcase that once stood in my grandfather's bedroom, which I was living in now. The bookcase had sagged almost entirely under the weight of the yellowed books and had always given the impression that it was just about to fall apart. This had happened every day for decades until it was finally thrown out without my knowledge, even before I had moved into my grandfather's flat.

I liked to take out a random book and admire its cover to the point of boredom, to search for every detail, to delve further, to check the year of publication and, more interestingly, the circulation. Those with the least circulation I valued the most, like greatest treasures. Especially if I couldn't take my eyes off the covers. This was the case with the books from PIW publishing house, which couldn't be mistaken for any other. Their books had pastel colors combined with a specific graphic style, which I cannot put into words, something like minimalism drawn by a child's hand, but also not entirely so. They were mainly just simplified illustrations – simple but not crude. What's more, they were almost always illustrations, rarely photos, and when they happened, they were usually modified, printed in strange colors, psychedelic ones.

Among all the books in the bookstores, there was probably not a single foreign book, only national classics, which were allowed to be published by the censors. I'm sorry, that's not entirely true, Homer was there, but that's about all of it.

I never saw my grandfather read any of the yellowed books from his shelf or even his slightest attention to them. They lay eternally covered with a thin layer of dust, waiting for me to pull out one of them and carefully blow the grayish shroud off it, trying not to sneeze, which was extremely hard to do. How this collection found its way to my grandfather is a mystery to me, which, unfortunately, I would never have the opportunity to unravel in this new world here.

I left the bookshop unnoticed, just as the books had left my grandfather's flat unnoticed one sad day after he had passed away from this world.

That said, the gifts had finally been bought. They were resting safely in the foil net, so I didn't see the point of my further presence in any of the stores. Instead, I wanted to enjoy the snowy weather, the outdoor nature, and real life.

There was also no point in going the same way I was going because I would have gone too far from home, and already, as I mentioned, I was out of my beloved neighborhood at the moment. On the horizon was the monstrous police headquarters building, which immediately reminded me of the first of my nightmares. It made me shudder at the mere thought of it. It would be better to go in a completely different direction and choose the next, more interesting point of pilgrimage, some nice place that would keep me in a good mood until dinner itself. I walked a few steps and having no idea where I should go next, I decided to get lost even for just a moment. It was an extremely difficult task considering that I have lived here since I was born and knew the city inside out.

Behind the bookstore and the adjoining parking lot, there was an uninhabited area of which there were little left in my town, the rest having been filled up with all the new money that had washed in. I struggled through a barren field, from which only frozen, broken weeds protruded, all of them bent down toward the ground as if they wanted to hide in it out of shame. My legs were falling into the depressions and unevenness of the ground over and over again. Fortunately, the snow was so cold that it didn't flow into my shoes. Along the way, I encountered more and more trees devoid of leaves, which more resembled the frozen weeds rather than any full-fledged trees. I walked forward at all time so that, if necessary, I could easily return the same way I had come.

Finally, I came across a small concrete road hidden between the broken trees of a small, sad forest. Although this forest must have been here continuously for several decades, if not centuries, as something ancient remaining in the city, it looked dwarfed, its trees warped and thin and not much larger than humans.

For some unknown reasons, they hadn't been able to rise higher, as if something in the soil wouldn't allow them to do so, pulling them back to the ground.A strange thought occurred to me that it's not because of the soil, but because these trees are ashamed of something. What can it be? A Cross was made of wood, but it was people who crucified the Savior. The wood didn't withstand the fire of subsequent bloody revolutions, but that was again the fault of the sinful human nature. Slave boats, weapons, instruments of torture, electric chairs, they are all man-made. I realized it's not a shame; the trees are afraid of human cruelty and greed. They prefer to suffer themselves than be the cause of suffering. They are real eternal Martyrs because Man is incapable of it... or it's just my naive imagination. One thing is for sure, finally they will be cut down to serve those they are afraid of.

The road that was hidden between this shadowy orchard of despair turned out to be perhaps the strangest in the city. Literally, along its entire length, it consisted of concrete slabs dug into the ground, which didn't touch each other and were separated by narrow strips of earth, like a continuous joint. It looked more like an abandoned military training ground than a place for relaxing walks with the family and yet it appeared that quite a lot of people visited it on weekends.

I had no idea when this path was last cleared and how all those blocks of concrete had been dug in there, but it must have been decades ago because the grass had already started to visibly rise up above the concrete, breaking it apart and gradually absorbing some of the slabs. I walked straight ahead, taking care not to trip over any chipped piece of concrete. This walk was definitely not one of the best pastimes I could have dreamed of. In such a place, for unknown reasons, you can always feel something primal, a mystery, or a strength that has been hidden for a long time.

After a while, I regretted that I had chosen this particular route, instead of simply returning to my neighborhood, where I had originally planned to spend my whole day. At this point, I might as well have walked across the street lamp-lit sidewalks instead of probing for holes that might break my ankles in the darkness. I also remembered where unfortunately this road leads. I wish I had thought about it right away before I had gotten there. But I didn't want to turn back, lest I meet Laura in such a mood by chance. The road ended exactly behind the hospital grounds, which I had already decided to avoid, in order not to risk meeting my ex-wife, not ready for this Day of Reconciliation.

About halfway down the strange broken road was an old brick house that looked more like a ruin than a place to live. It was separated from the road by a crooked wooden fence consisting of unpainted rails. Its end was nailed directly to the birch tree that grew on the corner of the land. There were no lights on in the windows and I would have supposed that nobody lived there anymore if it weren't for the barking of a wolfhound who was throwing furiously, chained somewhere behind the house. In the back, there was also a mysterious utility room, which seemed to be even older than the household. The only wall visible in the gloom was made of limestone and frightened with two narrow windows that had been boarded up. I must admit that it was a truly scary sight, which could scare you even on a bright, sunny day, and even moreso when it's dark, as it was getting. Instinctively, I quickened my pace, looking back from time to time to see if anyone was following me. The dog's bark still came from a distance. I wondered what might have been bothering it to such an extent.

From a distance, one could see the huge complex of hospital buildings, none of which had a good reputation. There were a lot of reportages recorded and publicly broadcast about its incompetent staff and the scandals that they had tried to cover up.

I walked under a huge overhead power line that likely powered half the neighborhood. The humming, which could be clearly heard, didn't stop for a moment and aroused even more anxiety in that I was almost in the dark. Finally, I made it to the maroon steel fence surrounding the huge landscaped area that belonged to the hospital. What surprised me were the four concrete posts to which live electrical wires had once been attached. These posts were standing mysteriously next to the actual fence. They evoked unpleasant memories for me, as they looked like they had been taken directly from a German death camp.

From this side of the buildings, only the driveway for ambulances and the entrance to the emergency room were visible, where there was almost always a queue, requiring people to wait several hours in their distress and discomfort. I had no desire to think about this place or the one right next to it as I associated it mainly with the stench of drunk people who were brought there after accidents, whose main cause was alcohol abuse. Falling down stairs was a daily occurrence.

When I was at the level of the side entrance, something tempted me to look in that direction, just only for a moment, and unfortunately, I saw there, the one who had tormented me in my dreams with her silence and her inhuman, insensitive smile. She was standing at the entrance to the Emergency Department smoking a cigarette with the doctor who had put his arm around her. I would never trust a smoking doctor. I'm not saying this out of envy, you can be sure about it. Luckily, she didn't notice me. She was busy staring at her phone screen despite the company.

I turned my head and walked on as if I had just seen a completely random stranger. I was well aware that any word said by one side or the other would be forced and insincere. We were strangers. It's hard to believe that it used to be different.

Until now, I have never wondered what would have happened if she hadn't disappeared from my life then. I didn't have time for those kinds of thoughts, taking care of Milena and working at the same time. But, as soon as I thought about it, I realized how lucky I was and what a torment it would be to have been in an eternal war at home, begging for her affection in front of a child, shouting and arguing, impermanent truces that would instantly turn into another inevitable war. It's very good that it happened, the disappearance. At first, I had felt that those memorable events were completely indifferent to me and, contrary to what I thought in this moment, I carried no regrets. What's more, all that time I was still under the strong impression of the meeting in the bookstore and I must admit that I had high hopes for it, finally feeling that I might be free from the traumas of the past.

I was walking straight ahead when, at the corner of the hospital square, where most of the staff cars were parked, I heard a sound.

Psst,

it came from behind a small woman's car, though the sound was clearly male.

I wondered if it was real, but after a while, the situation repeated.

Psst, here I am, come here, my friend.

I walked around the car and couldn't believe my eyes. Behind the car was crouched a gray, obese old Man in a thin ladies coat, which covered only his hospital pajamas.

Are you okay? Can I help you somehow?

I was concerned, thinking that I was dealing with a person suffering from Alzheimer's, as so much had been heard about them running away from homes, hospitals, and such.

No, my friend, everything is not okay,

the Man answered vaguely, without explaining anything.

What happened?

They won't let me be tanked, and you have to understand me, my friend, first-class booze is my life. It would be a sin not to drink. Don't you want to be blasted with me, my friend?

Please forgive me, but I believe that to be a rather bad idea.

And for the next one – the next problem that you asked about. They won't give me any morphine. Do you understand, my friend?

And what exactly is wrong with you?

My head hurts when I'm not drinking.

But you are drinking now...

You see, this is such a hospital that you have to heal yourself on your own. You have to prevent and be three steps ahead of everyone, otherwise, checkmate and after the game, they will wipe you off the board like any pawn, my friend.

You should probably go back inside, or you'll get pneumonia or something worse. There's no good reason to stay here longer than necessary.

What a smartass,

his tone changed in a second, and there was even a little bit of contempt in it, which surprised me greatly.

We already know that you aren't such a prude.

Wait, who's we? What do you mean?

I let him draw me into his game, which I soon regretted.

Who are we? Everybody. Angels, shepherds, and me,

his face contorting into a terrible grimace, which after a while, softened and the hostility disappeared from it.

Anyway, there is no need to be angry. Am I right, my friend?

Yes, you are,

I replied, wanting to avoid further trouble.

I'm just your friend, Phil, don't you want some vodka with me or a beer?

he said as he tried to persuade me by waving a dirty bottle right in my face.

I'm Stanley,

I introduced myself.

Please, forgive me, but as I mentioned, I'm a non-drinker. I don't have any addictions.

That means you have something to hide, Stan. I guess I can call you that, huh?

he laughed, and I felt even more awkward, which my interlocutor didn't appear to notice.

I didn't answer because the whole situation had long become too much for me, but the old man didn't seem to care. All the time he was talking just for the sake of talking. There are a lot of people like that in the world.

Would you like a car like this, my friend?

he pointed to the only car that I recognized at the time. I hadn't noticed it here before. It was a car I used to drive myself, and not with any fun. Strangely, she hasn't changed it yet.

Not necessarily, it reminds me of an ex-wife that I'd rather not remember,

I don't know why I confided in him to some extent, after all, he annoyed me from the very beginning, from the first words spoken.

I, however, would like to have it, for example, my friend. Wives are just wives, you can scare them with knives, you understand me, my friend, but me, I would sell this car and buy a better one,

he was babbling nonsense.

Who would you sell such an old car to? After all, it's about twenty-five years old and will sooner end up in scrap metal. It's just a piece of junk,

I discussed it with him, and I don't know why I did it.

You would be surprised. I can sell everything and everyone in a flash,

he went too far, but after these words, there was not a shred of evidence in him that might have indicated a slip of the tongue.

Maybe it's better to go back inside,

I tried again, fed up with this conversation.

I even wanted to take him to the hospital so he wouldn't freeze, but It was a hopeless case.

The first time I tried to grab his arm, but he pushed me with all his strength so that I almost fell over. He clenched his false teeth together, which was more comical than menacing. From then on, I chose to ignore him completely, regardless of his words or deeds. I moved to a safe distance, out of reach of his hands, and he continued to shout and called my name. He did this until hospital staff rushed to fetch him inside the building. From the faces of the newly arrived, it was clear that this wasn't the first time that the strange man had acted like that.

Hello, please stop. Where are you running to?

someone from the hospital staff shouted after me as they saw me heading towards the open space of more frozen, unsown fields.

I'm not running away anywhere, I'm just walking. Taking a walk is one thing that's still allowed in this country. You must have me confused with someone else.

This old man here,

he pointed to my new acquaintance, whom I'd rather have not met at all.

Claims that you escaped with him from the ward and forced him to drink alcohol in the cold.

And you believed him just like that?

Why would he lie? What would he get out of it?

How can I know? Maybe sick satisfaction, after all, he's insane!

I shouted in full frustration, completely fed up with similar situations.

And how can I know you're not a lunatic? You seem nervous.

You can't know it, but you can risk it and drag me to the ward by force, only for me to call the police right away. Do you want to risk such fun on Christmas Eve?

The Man was visibly confused. Almost everyone dreamed of returning home. It was better to take a chance, sweep any arguments under the rug and wait a few hours until they left work so that they could finally forget about everything.

Can you promise that you're not crazy?

I'm not going to promise anything, goodbye,

I told him and turned on my heel and headed in the opposite direction.

The Man who was trying to figure me out was stunned. He thought about what he heard for a moment, then he wrung his hands and decided to let me go. The whole convoy went into the warm hospital. No one was shouting anymore. Even the old Man was quite quiet and decent, which was unlike him. He understood that he couldn't win anything more and resignation took over.

Opposite the hospital, on the far right of the street, was a huge funeral home that looked more like a luxury villa than another old-fashioned industry establishments. This view certainly didn't fill the patients with optimism, the profit didn't come out of nowhere. I wasn't even going to go near this building, even though there was a shorter dirt road right behind it that led directly to my neighborhood. However, the lack of streetlights and the thicker layer of snow discouraged me even more from choosing this path, I would get wet all over.

My watch read almost half past three. I'd wound up the watch mechanism before I forget it so I'd know when to start going home. I expected that I still had some time before Milena returned from her friends. They hadn't seen each other for a long time, so there must have been quite a lot of topics to talk about.

It took me a whole hour to walk through the next two streets. It was a boring hour. There was nothing interesting about these streets. They looked like run-down suburbs, not as an integral part of the city with almost a quarter of a million citizens living in them every day. There were about forty-year-old houses with red tile roofs, lawns mowed only at the front of the property, and second-hand economy-class cars crammed into driveways piled with compacted dust. I had never been to this place before, and I felt as if I had seen it a thousand times, without much cordiality or delight.

I decided to find the nearest sign that would show me which way to return. It was high time for that – returning. I had had enough of my wanderings. I wanted to return to the places that had always been familiar and important to me, which I secretly considered to be a heritage received from my grandfather. I missed him very much.On Christmas Eve there was always a special feeling of missing loved ones who are no longer with us. It was high time to return home to Milena and the ever-living memories of the moments spent together with my grandfather. All I had to do was to finally find that one signpost, the way I came here was too long and complicated for me to get back on time.

Instead of the desired signpost, however, I saw the gate of the municipal cemetery. I hadn't the slightest idea that it could be reached by this road, I had never ventured that far into this area on foot before. There was a bus stop near the gate, so I decided to check the timetable. It was the final stop, so only buses of two lines left from there. Line 29 was the only one that ran through my neighborhood, though not directly across my street, but it wouldn't take long to get to it. I decided to go back home in this way, to have time to prepare a Christmas dinner. The only problem was that there was still almost an hour until the bus arrived.

I couldn't sit still; it was too cold not to be constantly moving. There was a large-sized brazier by the bus stop, but unfortunately, it was not fired, and I had no way to start a fire in it. I walked along the wall to bypass the main gate and warm up a bit by the way. When I reached the side gate, I saw a forest of crosses that grew out of granite monuments. It made a stunning impression on me, a person who had avoided cemeteries for years, just as much as I had avoided public hospitals. They both reminded me of sadness, death, and loneliness in equal measure.

It seemed that I haven't crossed any of the gates of the municipal cemetery for a good dozen or so years. The last time I was here was for my mother's funeral, which appeared to me only as a movie projected behind a thick pane of glass. I know that I'm not very precise at this point, but someone who has never experienced the feeling of derealisation himself won't be able to fully imagine such a phenomenon. Maybe it wasn't any derealisation, but overtiredness or a clumsy attempt at feelings that were no longer in me. Maybe it was indifference.

In the same cemetery, a few alleys away, in a small wooden box, there was an urn with my grandfather's ashes. I admit that so far, I hadn't paid much attention to it either, but for completely different reasons. I believed that my grandfather was in a better world, enjoying the presence of God, freed from material needs, and hunger, and therefore there was no reason to worry about His earthly ashes.

For so many years, I used to speak in monologues to my grandfather every day before falling asleep, as if he could hear me and be glad that He was present in my life. Every year, I sent a letter addressed to the Kingdom of Heaven, but I never expected the post office to deliver any of them. Maybe if I knew the postal code it would have been different. I'm curious about what happened to all these letters after sending them because I didn't indicate the sender to whom the letters could be returned to if they couldn't be delivered.

I opened the steel gate and dove into a world that had always been strange to me. The darkness was illuminated by thousands of candles, and shadows danced with the winds on the icy slabs of marble and granite. I tried to remember where my grandfather's grave was. It seemed to me that I knew roughly the direction in which I should go, but I assumed that I could be wrong.

I decided to visit this grave, although I didn't believe in any of the magical powers of cemeteries or in their uniqueness. The deceased, even if they stayed in another world, were indifferent to the burial place of their corpses and how many candles and bouquets would be on their monuments. For years, there had been an informal cemetery fashion competition and an outdoing in the number of ornaments on a tombstone. Paradoxically, those of the living who had the most sins on their conscience bought the most for their dead, as if they wanted to justify themselves to the rest of the world, unable to repair their wrongs. Despite considering most of these things as hypocrisy, I decided to end my pilgrimage in this very place, which many associated with the end of everything.

Passing numerous monuments on the way, I looked at the engraved oval portraits as if I were about to meet someone familiar, so kind of a face that, though made of stone, would become a part of my life for a moment, and would then be resurrected by my imagination, only to become absent again after a while to the people of the temporal world. Most of the people in these photographs were dressed in old-fashioned clothes, as the tombstone

portraits had already started to go out of fashion and cur-
rently few families opted for them. That's what made them
catch my eye. These pictures said so much more than the
names, surnames, or dates of birth and death. Every few
steps I slowed to get a better look at their suits, uniforms,
or ball gowns. All the elegance was distorted, only temporary in earthly life, and yet only it seemed to be appropriate
when it came to immortalizing someone.

To reach the one monument, I had to force my way
through a veritable Crowd that spread evenly over the entire
surface of the main alley. The annual tradition ordered people to come to the cemetery not only on All Saints' Day or
All Souls' Day but also on this day, Christmas Eve, which
should have been associated primarily with the expectation
of a birth.

The main diagonal alley was arched, dividing the cemetery into two parts. It was the only division between the
people who rested there. But perhaps there were more, even
more insignificant.

The mighty, trick oaks, which even three people couldn't
surround with their arms, were the main perpetrators of this
turmoil. If they had had memory, it would date back to the
times of establishing the cemetery and its first burials. Wit-
nessing the passing of several human generations, they had
managed to sprout roots long enough to intertwine together
underground in and among the buried dead, creating a for-
mation resembling a neural network of sorts. Under the
pressure from the roots, some of the graves were lifted, and
others were slowly sinking. There was no solution other than

cutting down the trees, which was ultimately not decided to be done.

The huge pile of garbage under the fence grew regularly. It was a pile that wouldn't fit into the large blue dumpster next to it because it was already full. Out of the rotten grass, the last swath of the year that hadn't been cleared away, cracked plastic shells of burnt candle holders emerged. The damp, cool air was conducive to the spread of the smell of dried stearin mixed with the aroma of drying flower bunches and the aforementioned rotten grass, whose frost prevented its complete decomposition. A faucet, which protruded from the well that was supposed to provide water for washing the monuments, was decorated by nature with an icicle that reached the very ground. You might even think it was growing out of the ground like a strange winter flower.

I had no problems finding a grave with a name close to mine, though I hadn't been here for a dozen or so years. When I got there, I realized that Milena must have been here today as well. The monument had been cleared and a small red candle was burning on it. I never saw the point in burning all these lamps, but despite everything, I felt warm at the thought that I was not the only one who remembers someone who had raised me, someone whom I still love very much, even though he has not been with me for some twenty-five years. Many will consider it naive, but I believe that we will meet again and I'm not ashamed of it.

Milena had no right to meet my grandfather in person, but she loved him because of my stories and because he meant so much to me. I had taken Milena to this place only once, when she was still small, the more I was surprised that she remembered the way to the resting place of her great-grandfather's ashes, the ashes of a man with as big a heart who had used it for his loved ones and cheerfully didn't care about the rest of the world.

Despite the general Crowd, the alley where my grandfather's grave was located is almost deserted. I looked around to make sure again that I could count on privacy. Everything pointed to the fact that I could.

Frost pinched my cheeks mercilessly, just like on that memorable day of the December funeral. I remember today a narrow but not very deep pit into which a small wooden box was lowered with everything that was left of my grandfather's body, the person whom I admired the most, loved, and still love so much. I remember how the cold cracked the skin of my hands and they began to ooze blood, which dripped to the ground and mixed with the frozen, dark earth. That cold, however, couldn't compare with the cold and emptiness I had within myself, standing stiffly in front of the unfilled grave, throwing a handful of earth on the lid of the miniature coffin, responding with only a dull thud.

I remember the few anxious faces. Most faces were indifferent or falsely sad so as not to appear awkward in front of the rest of the gathering, some of them glancing frantically at their watches from under their exposed sleeves, wanting to run away but not able to do it. They all would go with their lives as if nothing had changed. On that same day, everything was hidden under the marble, just as unwanted lint for which a man doesn't even want to stoop, is swept under the carpet. It's covered and there's no problem and one can safely pretend that it never existed.

Everyone went their separate ways, returning to the everyday matters or simply in front of theirKinescopes, allowing them to forget about the details of real life.

If I had been buried alive there that day, I wouldn't have objected. I would have watched the ground sleepily cover me more and more without giving the slightest warmth. Was it that quiet then, or did my memory deceive me? I remembered a funeral song about an angelic procession sung without enthusiasm by a group of mourners and instinctively, like a child, I looked to the sky, as if it was supposed to hide these heavenly hosts that would come down at any moment to visit the people.

I remembered the poor little Angel-like Boy who had escaped from the exhibition area to go on his way, but there was no trace of him in the sky and he was nowhere to be found.

The sky was cloudless anyway. Maybe two or three feathery clouds obscured some of the constellations that decorated the horizon for all generations back when that could be remembered. The moon, in its cheeky, characteristic way, stood out in the foreground, outshining the rest of the celestial bodies, which seemed to be only a background created especially for its needs. Rocky craters, reminders of the many victorious battles upon its surface, clearly visible from so far, seemed to be within a stone's throw. It must be freezing up there. A frozen, empty lump, like the many unused human hearths. If the moon had a nationality, it would probably be

French and wear a Napoleonic hat. It would tempt us with its charm and chic, but for us, it would still be an unfamiliar charm, reflected back like those of sunbeams. It was tempting to knock it out of the sky that or any evening and stop this delicious parade going on from time immemorial.

It was the first time that I didn't care at all to leave this place that held the remains of so many people who might have been related to me in one way or another and I didn't even know it. In full consciousness, I had long been ready to join their ranks.

During the visit described, I had something to live for, despite frequent complaints and a lot of everyday problems, which were nothing in face of disease, hunger, war, or death. You could say that I still had a better time than half of humanity, and that's probably a pretty good result. I wanted to share this change for the better with my grandfather, to rejoice together, albeit temporarily separately. I looked around again to make sure no one had come near. The alley was empty. The older parts of the cemetery were less frequently visited, and over time the memory of each of their ancestors passed irretrievably among everyday life. But I didn't forget.

Hi Grandpa. How are you today? I hope you are happy in the place you are now and that you are not feeling lonely. I also don't want you to worry because there's no reason to do so. December always reminds me of your baggy gray diamond pattern sweater, which you probably do not need anymore. I can't imagine that you have to worry about Winter in the Eternal Life, although on the other hand, sometimes it's nice to feel a refreshing coolness that reminds you of the reality of what surrounds us. It seems more real to me what we have already experienced, the time of childhood with you when I wasn't concerned by the need to earn money to ensure that my family will survive, but now that's unfortunately necessary. I also have beautiful moments, even every day, when it's a quiet evening and dinner time in our flat. My family, you, and Milena are everything to me. I miss you but don't worry about it, after all, every day brings us closer to meeting again. Maybe we'll even live in one place, the whole family together if that's possible.

I can't imagine what the Kingdom of Heaven looks like, but if I had to choose, it would look exactly like our district, which strangely would contain any number of people or objects, although you probably don't have any objects at all. There would be the same birch trees and weeping willows and the hill I sled down as a kid. Christmas is fast approaching for us here and I appreciate that I will spend it with Milena, your great-granddaughter. It's a pity that you never had the opportunity to meet her in person, it was so close with only a few years between you two. I'm sure that you would have liked each other, and maybe even loved each other. I'm sure it will be that way, take my word for it.

Too bad you're not here with us. I'm sorry if I repeat myself and talk about the same things every day, but lately, there hasn't been much going on. Well, maybe today something changed. Maybe you already know everything, but it's always nice to tell you about the things that are important to me.

Milena found the watch you gave me when I was a child. Do you remember it, Grandpa? It is such a small thing, and I can't remember ever receiving a better gift. It made me visit some places that I remembered from our good times, but I veered off track, got lost, and ended up here by accident, even though you know I don't like places like that. Along the way, I met a boy who didn't seem to have much luck. I hope it won't be, but if he comes here, Grandpa, please look after him this Christmas and apologize to him for me, I really couldn't help him as much as I had wanted to. What am I talking about? I'm sure he will be fine, and as always, I worry unnecessarily. I'm always doing this, it's time to stop it.

On the other hand, on to more pleasant things, I met a nice girl today... a woman. People always feel young, and immortal until the very end. Maybe it's funny, but I still feel like a twenty-year-old, or maybe I just felt old then. Who knows? Returning to the topic, my nice revelation is called Laura and I'm hoping something will come of it, though maybe I'm being too positive. I don't want to be disheartened. I felt like this for the first time in some twenty years. I realize that the beginnings are always sweet and fantastic, and then you have to face the real-life problems and consider all the pros and cons about a person.Please wish me luck, Grandpa. It was you who taught me that it's never too late to be happy. I Now believe that you were right. I love you Grandpa and thank you for raising me. Thank you for every moment together and every kind word. Thank you just for being you. I hope you're at least a little proud of me. Have a nice day, Grandpa, see you in the Kingdom of Heaven, or so I hope.

When I told my grandfather about my day almost like every day, as if he could hear me, I felt relieved. I felt like he was somewhere within reach and was thinking of me in a caring way. I prayed for a while more, this time in silence. I rubbed my cold hands to warm them a bit and slowly made my way to the exit.

Without knowing why, I decided to see what I would feel when I stood again in front of my mother's grave, which I hadn't seen since the funeral, in front of that cold marble slab with the surname that is also mine.

There were fewer visitors to the monuments; everyone was rushing home to get ready for the visits of other, less important, family members, which were to take place before the actual Christmas Eve dinner. There was still about half an hour until the bus that I needed to take arrived. Because I had no one to visit, I didn't have to hurry or overpay for a taxi. Milena was probably still with her friends, and I didn't want to be at home alone, risking a bad mood on such a special day. So, I still had a bit of time.

It took me a while to find the grave in the farther, newer part of the cemetery, where all the graves were almost identical and crammed together for lack of space to further expand the boundaries.

I stood in front of it, the grave of the person from whose stigma I couldn't fully free myself even many years after her death. Could it be her invisible hand from the beyond that tricked me here to test me? I expected the worst, the release of accumulated emotions that I could subconsciously suppress for years, tears, screams, and all. But, nothing of the sort happened at all. I didn't feel anger or regret. I wasn't paralyzed by fear or stress. Maybe it's a shame, but instead, I was struck by a simple, utter indifference, as if the whole thing was about a stranger or pure abstraction. I decided not to mention it to anyone, not even Milena, and this time I really headed for the exit gate. There was nothing else to keep me there. It was too beautiful to live.

Cold, I went to the bus stop and sat on an old bench with the paint peeling off. There were ten minutes left before the scheduled arrival of the bus. To make time more pleasant, I admired the drawings on the glass that must have been made by children returning from the cemetery that very day. They had decorated the surface of almost the entire glass side wall of the bus stop. I saw no sadness or fear in the drawings, which made me smile. They were full of snowmen, snowflakes, hearts, and names, but no deaths, breakups, or addictions. Like a child, I was delighted with this primitive mosaic filled with optimism. I stared at it until the arrival of the aforementioned bus of line twenty-nine driving towards Witold Gombrowicz Street, who is my favorite writer anyway.

My red-chilled ears were attacked by the squeak of the bus door opening, so familiar was it to me from the one from my childhood. Absolutely nothing has changed, nothing ever does. I had come across one of the last shabby relics of public transport from the times when it was still the main means of transport for most of society. Thirty years ago, almost no family could afford the luxury of having a car. Now it's difficult to park anywhere, not only in the city center but also in the smaller districts. I struggled up the high, muddy steps into the insides of the bus and smelled the smell of exhaust fumes, a small amount of which must have entered into the interior through the leaky windows.

There was not a single passenger inside except me, and the driver himself was quite hidden in his built-up cab, which was decorated with a pennant from the outside. From behind the photos in my wallet, I pulled out a ticket that I always carried with me, as was the old habit, "just in case," even though I hadn't used public transport in years. I hoped that the ticket price hadn't been raised and that it wouldn't put me at risk of the dubious pleasure of being ticketed on Christmas Eve. On the other hand, I was aware of the ever-progressing inflation, almost all prices in the stores went up and there was no sign of this unpleasant trend reversing. I decided to take a chance and not check the current price, not wanting to chat with a stranger. The ticket puncher was suitable for a museum of technology; it was an old type with teeth that pierced the ticket with a grunt. I sat down in the penultimate row, on a soft, though firmly used seat. It was covered with holes in the dark brown leather. Jagged sponges protruded from these holes, probably placed inside the seat originally by the manufacturers themselves.

My grandfather had been a professional bus driver for most of his life, and I was riding a bus for the first time since he left this world. On a bus that he might once have driven himself, though there was no way of knowing if that was true. Maybe it's strange or even quite infantile, but I felt like he was there with me, watching over me and letting me know that he still loved me and was waiting for me wherever he is now. A tear ran down my cheek, a good tear that only my daughter could lure out of hiding and now my beloved grandfather could bring to my eyes. At that moment, I felt calmer, relaxed, and filled with inner warmth and goodness. Finally, I was able to go home.

The pleasant, nostalgic thoughtfulness lasted a few good minutes, and when I focused on the view through the window, I saw that I was also only a few minutes drive from the bus stop where I had originally intended to get off.

On all sides the horizon was covered with oblong blocks of flats and college buildings, once gray and stark, now in all kinds of pastel colors and shades of green, most of which I couldn't name. All the birch trees, which dominated over all the other trees in this area, were in contrast to the rainbows made of the large building blocks. Someone influential must have had a real soft spot for them when my district was founded. It's probably worth mentioning that my district was founded decades ago on the occasion of the thousandth anniversary of the creation of the Polish state, hence its name. Over the decades, the once birch saplings have managed to match the blocks in terms of height, and in many cases even surpass them, and overtake them in the race for the most eye-catching color.

The wheels of the bus rolled slowly to another glass bus stop. Again, there was a familiar squeal of the doors opening that I haven't heard since.

I got off the bus two stops before the one closest to my block because I decided to visit one more place before the official end of my pilgrimage. Something made me want to end it on a positive note, just like I had started it. The cemetery didn't seem like a proper end to me, neither to the pilgrimage nor life in general, it couldn't end just like that.

Immediately, I was refreshed by the pleasant, moist air that escaped from me in the form of steam. Again, I was at the tram line, at a huge crossroad. On the other side of the street was a series of buildings of the academy and the polytechnic, the one which Milena attended. Waiting for the light to turn green was boring for me, but I finally made it safely across through the zebra crossing and passing both of the academy buildings that were right next to it. It was hidden just behind them, the unique place that from time to time attracted me with its history.

Hoffman's Villa from the 18th century was the almost forgotten beginning of my beloved district. It is a small palace with an impressive dome, hidden away behind a crooked fence and overgrown weeds. The windows and doors have long ago been boarded up so as not to tempt the homeless and local youth to visit it. Once in a while, however, someone burst inside, wanting to know its mysterious, tempting interior. In the past, the villa was the home of a landowner, a passionate fruit grower who even had some precursory achievements in this field. Trees and bushes once covered most of the district and its Pearl was the magnificent rosarium located behind the palace at the time. Today, the Rose

Garden is only a distant past, of which there are no photographs, but it's nice to imagine a marriage who first walked among the flowers in the summer with their children.

It is said that the evangelical community bought the villa and part of its land, only to sell it after years of inactivity to a developer who bought it only to build the office building next to it. Nevertheless, Hoffman's Villa stayed here as I did, regardless of the passing time and the changes that were taking place around. Abandoned and neglected, it delighted everyone who wandered and stumbled across it with its aging beauty. Few inhabitants of the city knew about its existence, but those who had the honor of knowing its secret never forgot about it. This is probably where it all began when it comes to the history of the district I love, the district where my grandfather lived and died, and the district where I was born and will probably leave this world.

Contact with the past, with the roots, made me feel uplifted, and any negative emotions have long since disappeared from me. I felt an incredible weightlessness inside me as if I weighed only five kilograms and the slightest gust of wind could carry me towards the familiar streets where I had grown up. I was feeling drunk, and yet I hadn't drunk a drop.

It was dusk outside. I narrowed my eyes as I passed the row of street lamps, and their numerous rays of light began to dance and spin for me, inviting me to play together. I felt the joy of a child as I walked home, expecting to find Milena, my daughter, there.

It was only a few blocks from here, and the sidewalks were deserted as if the world had come to an end. Everyone had sat down with their families at tables or packed their cars and headed for their loved ones, only to get stuck in traffic jams. My pilgrimage had taken me much longer than I had originally planned, but I hoped that I would make it home on time and together with Milena we would finish the preparations together.

I returned to the height of the rails, where the black cat lurked in the grass for its hidden victim. It had something of human nature in it. The hangman didn't kill its victim right away, but he played with it cruelly. The claws didn't dig in, but tossed the body of the poor animal. The gray mouse squealed in panic, begging for mercy. I tried to chase the cat away but it hissed angrily and came back to tormenting the victim. The tram was coming so I had to go. The mouse was out on a limb and I felt guilty. I passed the cat, careful not to lose my head like Berlioz, and jumped into the second wagon. I punched the last ticket I managed to dig out of my wallet, again ignoring the risk of changing prices.

An urban legend told that checks always only took place in the front wagon. There were a few people in the wagon apart from me, and the tram rocked us side to side as if secretly trying to lull us to sleep. Two stops filled with rattling and I was almost near to the destination place. It was enough to cross the street, which I did.

Before entering the staircase, I stopped for a moment and looked at the already-mentioned birch trees that have been growing in this place for as long as I can remember.

The birch branches, covered with wet snow, looked as if they were covered with catkins. They looked as if they were preparing to give new life with their delicate, thin leaves.

I climbed the staircase and carefully wiped my shoes on the doormat by the intercom. The front door was so loose that it could be opened without a key. All you had to do was to put anything in the right place of the wide gap and the lock would give up, allowing anyone to enter. The staircase was full of smells, there was a buzz everywhere. Christmas preparations were in full swing. Only my apartment was quiet, but I was hoping for a quick change of situation related to the return of my daughter.

I climbed the stairs. As soon as I turned the key in the lock, I got a wonderful surprise. Milena opened the door and threw herself into my arms with a charming smile on her face. She must have been waiting for me for some time because her cheeks were no longer flushed, which always happened to her in the cold and would last up to thirty minutes after entering the house. After all, everything was as it should always be. I hung up my flat cap on the hook, took off my coat, and managed to make another smile with the sweater she gave me last year.

Hi sweetie!

Hi dad, merry Christmas!

Thank you very much for finding my grandfather's watch. It's the most beautiful gift I've ever received, now both from him and you, so it's doubly special.

I'm glad that you are happy, dad.

You don't even know how much.

By the way, you could wind up your watch and look at it more often, it's almost seven o'clock. Where have you been all this time? Anyway, don't worry, we'll make it. I already managed to prepare part of the dinner by myself.

I would like to tell you everything when we sit down at the table together, but I don't know if you will believe everything, because I have a problem with it myself. In the meantime, we can finish the preparations. I'll help you with the rest. I just want to ask you something first,

I decided to break through.

What's up dad? Has something serious happened?

my little Angel was worried.

No, you have absolutely nothing to worry about. Everything is absolutely fine. I… I just…

Come on now, dad, don't be like that. Don't make me guess, you know I don't like it. Anyway, I'm a woman, you have no right to do that.

Okay, I met someone,

when I said that I felt like the huge burden had been lifted. Now all that was left was to wait for Milena's reaction, there was no turning back.

You mean some woman?

Yes, some woman, but I'm not sure yet and I would like you to tell me what you think about it.

Yeah, finally. I thought it would never happen. I'm so happy,

she replied with undisguised joy.

What is she like? Tell me.

Actually, I don't know much about her yet. I just got her number. I preferred to ask you first.

So, what are you waiting for dad? Go and call her, she's probably waiting for it. It is Christmas Eve, and nobody wants to sit alone,

she was getting more and more excited, gesticulating lively, and almost jumping with joy, which positively surprised me. I didn't expect her to be so happy.

I took my daughter's advice and immediately went to call the number written on the piece of paper.

One signal...

two signals...

I thought that no one would pick up when suddenly I heard this voice hypnotizing with its sweet timbre and gentleness.

Hello?

Good evening, you gave me this number in the bookstore today and I decided that there was no point in waiting any,

I said, trying not to reveal the anxiety that came over me, although it seemed like an impossible task.

Oh, it's you, Sir, I'm glad you're calling. I didn't want to mess up.

Please don't call me "Sir", my name is Stanley.

Of course, Sir. Oh, I'm sorry, it's not so easy to switch. I'm Laura, yes, indeed it will be better this way.

I think so. What do you think about going for a walk or to a coffee shop tomorrow? I suggest Under the Parrots at ten AM. Is it okay for you?

All right,

she said with real satisfaction in her voice.

What books should I take with me?

Sorry, but I don't understand what you mean, could you clarify?

I was confused because I didn't suspect reading together.

I have an employee discount and I sell books cheaper, under the counter, unfortunately without a receipt, but they are new and fragrant. Wasn't that the point from the beginning?

I'm sorry Mrs. Laura, I must have misunderstood your intentions. It was me who fooled myself.

Mrs. Laura? I thought we were on a first-name basis.

I'm sorry, you are right.

And you weren't fooled at all. Well, maybe a little bit by believing in this not very funny joke. Of course, it was all about a date. I don't even have an employee discount, although I must admit, it would come in handy, maybe I would finally earn something

Do you tell the truth?

Yes, I do; I could really use that discount,

she laughed, which already completely dispelled the earlier mood of uncertainty.

So, see you tomorrow?

I wanted to make sure though.

Yes, see you tomorrow.

I order Iwaszkiewicz and Witkiewicz.[3]

---

[3] Famous Polish writers of 20th century

Well, noted. I need to check availability then, you made me do it, so bye-bye in the meantime.

I'll pay by card, see you later,

I replied, and she hung up after a dozen or so seconds, during which we listened to each other's breathing, or at least mine certainly was like that.

Everything went well and as I mentioned, I was successful in making an appointment for the next morning. A first date on Christmas has to be something unforgettable. We chose the nearby promenade as the meeting place, with a park and lots of small squares with benches and even chess tables. From the very morning, almost everything was going wonderfully and I began to believe that this happiness would never leave me except the working time, but I had no impact on that, so I decided not to worry about it and let myself focus only on the bright side of life.

Milena was already waiting for news. It was obvious that she couldn't find a place for herself and bustled around the room, from one corner to the other.

How did it go? Will you get married? Will I have to call her mom?

she burst out with a series of questions, obviously delighted because she knew me very well and could read everything from my face before I said anything. I also didn't hide my satisfaction.

Well... Maybe... No...

I replied, emphasizing each word and teasing slightly.

We'll see each other again tomorrow morning.

We have to plan everything. Do you have an ironed shirt?

I think so.

A jacket for New Year's Eve would also be useful because you are going to invite her, aren't you?

Before I had time to answer, I suddenly heard a mysterious splash behind me. Milena smiled, though she was confused.

See for yourself,

she anticipated my question, not wanting to reveal the secret, which I didn't insist on, being able to check everything myself at once. Curious, I entered the bathroom and saw the cause of all the commotion in the bathtub.

There was a huge carp that was swimming tirelessly back and forth as if looking for a secret way to go home. I'm not exaggerating about its size, I'm not an angler and I have no interest in it. Its scales cut through the water, and it didn't seem to get tired of all that constant swirling. For reasons unknown to me, I felt some kind of respect for this fish, although perhaps it's better to describe it as an admiration for nature that almost every human has had since the very beginning. I went closer to get a good look at its flexible movements, and that's when it saw me with its fishy, innocent eyes, which seemed to portray sadness and an almost human understanding of the situation in which it found itself.

We weren't an average, statistical family, and although we loved Christmas traditions, we never bought carp for Christmas Eve, let alone Christmas Day, so I was even more surprised by its unusual presence under our roof. I glanced questioningly at my daughter, hoping she would explain our new tenant's move-in after all.

I got it as a gift from a friend, or rather from her parents, and I was stupid enough to accept it. I hope you are not angry that I took it. I didn't want to make anyone sad.

Of course, I'm not angry. You didn't do anything wrong. The only thing is that we have a new colleague on our hands and someone needs to take care of it.

What will we do with it? It's so helpless dad,

she showed her selfless kindness that I always liked so much and which could make me feel better in a flash.

I don't think we have a choice and we have to…

I stopped to see Milena's changing face and immediately decided not to cause her further uncertainty.

Let it go free, but only in the morning because it is a long way to the river. Also, it's too late today, let us see what it tells us at midnight.

Thank you, dad. I knew I could count on you.

Of course, we can also keep this carp if you promise to take it for walks.

I was traumatized enough from my childhood when every year the same fish ended up on the table and not back into the river. To this day, I remember the scene when, at the age of seven, my mother took me to the tub, showed me a carp, and handed me a rolling pin to stun, kill and gut the fish. I was unable to do so. Instead of killing the carp, I stood there for half an hour staring at its gills and its mouth, which kept moving, as if asking for mercy, for the right to live. Unfortunately, it wasn't heard then. My mother and a neighbor, seeing that I was still staring at the fish, pulled the plug of the tub, and the fish began to suffocate in front of my eyes on that Christmas afternoon. In the evening it was placed on a plate over which an official prayer was said. There, I secretly prayed for its soul, because to this day I believe that all living creatures have it, not only just humans. I decided to save my daughter from such events as well as my story about them.

We returned to the living room buoyed by our common resolution. I was surprised at how many things my daughter managed to deal with while waiting for my return because she was here only about half an hour before me. If I had known this was going to happen, I would have returned much sooner to help her. I was immensely proud of my grown-up daughter who was becoming so resourceful.

Our old oak table was already set and there was still a warm dinner on it, which was high time because the first star had already shone in the sky. And, according to the old Polish tradition, Hay was hidden under the tablecloth, and there was an additional chair at the table, which was to remind me of my grandfather, with whom Christmas had something magical and elusive. On the wall of the living room, there is a photo that shows me and my grandfather celebrating Christmas together.

I lit a candle, took the Holy Bible in my hands and we began to read, as every year, a fragment of the Gospel According to Saint Luke about the Birth of the Saviour, the shepherds, and the Angel.

When we finished reading, we smiled at each other and Milena hugged me just like she did as a little girl. I felt very moved again on this one special day. I wanted it to never end. I wanted to close it like in a snow globe, to stay in the perfect microcosm that I had been dreaming about for years. We took the Wafer in our hands and broke it in half.

Since you were born, everything has become better, and everything has more sense than before. Thank you for being you. For me, you are a real miracle. I wish you to always meet good, kind, and selfless people on your way. The world can be a wonderful place when you have people like that by your side. I love you baby girl and I'm very proud of you.

Thank you for saying that dad, you have no idea how much it means to me. I love you too, more than life itself, and I appreciate everything you do for me every day. I appreciate that you are always good, patient, and gentle. I wish you the same and that you can have more free time and rest, because you deserve it like no one else, and I would love to spend more time with you too.

We swallowed the broken pieces of the wafer and embraced. When it was time to eat, we poured warm compote from a jug and were about to sit down at the table, when suddenly someone knocked loudly on the door.

So it happened, and for the first time in the history of this house, an unannounced guest showed up. I was shocked. Maybe it's a shame, but I can't say that I was happy about the unexpected visit. Milena looked at me searchingly, probably expecting a planned surprise, but quickly realized that nothing of the sort happened.

The first person that came to my mind was my ex-wife, but I quickly abandoned this thought because she never showed up, she was absent even at Milena's birthdays during the times that we were together. After all, I had just seen her by chance at work, and she would never quit sooner – work was her whole life, her real obsession. My second suspicion was that it was the poor little boy whom I met at the exhibition, which I would have been glad of, but it was impossible, because he didn't know the address, and it was also impossible for him to have followed me for so long and meandering. I did hope that he had found a good place to spend the evening; I was very concerned about that. I hoped he wasn't freezing to death in a snowdrift somewhere. I decided I would attempt to find him tomorrow, although I didn't know yet how I would do it and how I could actually help him. Surely, he has parents and I couldn't just take him with me; no one would allow it. I had to give it some serious thought, but for now, I had to deal with the newcomer.

I suddenly began to feel the worst about the figure behind the door, though I couldn't figure out who it was. I stood numb and didn't move from where I was, which surprised my Angel as well. The knock on the door repeated, so it couldn't be a coincidence.

Don't worry dad, someone's probably just collecting money.

You are probably right,

I snapped out of my thoughts.

I'll check who it is. Maybe there are only some poor sect members. Nowadays, there are more and more of them; people are lost and looking for any hope.

Don't bother dad. Sit down, I'll check it. Maybe it's someone for me.

She took the first step and approached the door. She opened it without first asking about the visitor's identity.

What I saw left me stunned, it was a shock that I had never experienced before, and I had already seen many things that I would rather forget. He was standing in the doorway, the vile creature.

Good morning, would there be a place for me in the house of such a wonderful lady?

he said without any shame to Milena and reached out his disgusting hand to take the beautiful and innocent hand he was unworthy of. That day the animals did indeed speak with a human voice, though it was hard to call it that.

Unable to bear the insult, I sprang to my feet, grabbed the first thing I had at hand, and hid it behind my back. From the specific shape, I recognized that it was a knife with a mermaid-shaped handle, which had always served as an ornament in my grandfather's apartment. I approached our visitor.

He looked me straight in the eye, and I read the mockery on his face. So, he was playing with poor dad's feelings.

Good evening, my name is Stanley and...

he didn't manage to finish and collapsed at my feet in surprise as if begging for forgiveness.

It hadn't lasted long though.

Everything is finally gone.

I dropped the knife and couldn't take my eyes off my bloodstained hands.

Drip drip, drip drip, like a funeral march.

2022, Tysiąclecie, Częstochowa

AUTHOR BIO

Damian Pasieka is a Polish novelist debuting in his first English language novel with Montag Press. He is a proud father of his two sons, Jan and Witold. Parenthood, literature, and chess are his biggest passions. He graduated from Jan Długosz University in Częstochowa.

www.ingramcontent.com/pod-product-compliance
Lightning Source LLC
Chambersburg PA
CBHW030255270626
47156CB00022B/2761